The Woodsman's Boy

April Blanchard

April Blanchard

Cover design and typography: Matt Blanchard

Thanks to Matt Blanchard for formatting and providing cover art for this book, to Mick Jarvis, basket maker, for use of his pack basket and buffalo plaid jacket, and to Joel Lamphear and Dale Langlois for advice about trapping.

Dedicated to the memory of my parents,
Carol Fish Blanchard and Ernie Blanchard,
two true Adirondack characters.

Things you must know before reading this novel

Many of the characters in this novel really lived in the Adirondacks, but because this is fiction and I am far too young to have met these people, I have made up the situations and conversations.

There are some unpleasant attitudes toward people of other races and economic fortune portrayed in this book as well as hunting practices that are now illegal. Because these things are a part of our history, and this is an historical novel, I felt they had to be included.

April Blanchard

THE WOODSMAN

CHAPTER ONE

I ran home through the rain, holding my school books under my coat and dodging the horse-drawn carriages and carts that bounced over the cobbled London streets. Our butler answered my ring, and I slipped quickly through the door and set my books on the hall table. "It's raining outside, Hardwick," I said as I shed my dripping coat and pulled off my boots.

"So I see, William." He lowered his voice a bit. "You would be wise to tread softly today, your grandmother has received a letter."

I nodded. "Thanks for the warning," I whispered. I decided to skip my usual afternoon greetings and go straight to my room to study. I knew my grandmother would be in a bad temper and I wanted to put off seeing her until dinner. Passing through the parlor on the way to the staircase, I stopped to look at the two photos on the mantle. One was of a tall, grave looking young soldier, Uncle John, who lived in New York and had written the letter Hardwick had warned me about. The other was a photo of my mother dressed for her coming out ball. She had died nine years before, when I was born. There was no picture of my father. The only image I had of him was the dark one my own mind conjured up. He lived in New York too but not in the city.

I was almost to the stairs when my grandmother came through the door from the dining room. She had a look on her face that would have warned me even if Hardwick hadn't.

"William, you will be pleased to hear that I have just received a letter from your Uncle John, and he and his family are all doing very well. Your Aunt Hope has given birth to a baby boy, and they are both healthy. They will name the baby Laurence after your grandfather." She looked up at the picture of my mother and sighed. "Your mother would be alive today if she had married a reasonable man. And she had so many to choose from. Such a beautiful and obedient girl." She gave me a fierce look, so different from the calm and loving expression she usually had. "Your father was a smooth and tricky man. He promised her so much. He was lazy, a cowardly fool, and cared for nothing but his mountains and his uncivilized way of life.

I'd heard it all before, so I fidgeted and looked toward the stairway, longing to escape to my room, but my grandmother didn't notice, she kept on with her tirade.

"He took your mother into the woods where there were no stores or roads or even any other women, just a few men and Indians, as wild as your father or worse. It was a terrible place for a woman."

Every time she told this story I pictured a squat cabin set up against an outcropping of rock. Dark, thickly set fir trees ringed the front and there was a lock on the door. Bars were at the windows and my mother stood looking out between them with her ball gown on.

My grandmother went on, "When your mother was expecting you I begged him to bring her back to the city. He finally did, but it was not in a carriage or even on a horse that he brought her. It was on foot. He walked her out. At a time when most women are lying in, waiting for a child, your mother was being dragged on foot through the woods like an Indian. He did it to spite me. It's a wonder you survived and no wonder that she did not." She stopped, looked again at the pictures and then at me and sighed. She turned to go and said, "You had best be at your studies. There is plenty of time between now and dinner."

I always wondered what there was about a letter from Uncle John that set her off on the subject of my father. She loved her son. It was an idea I had that letters from him reminded her how far she was from home. Both she and my grandfather disliked London and were there only to keep me from my father. My grandparents felt exiled, but London was my home and I loved it.

I went up to my bedroom and sat down with my Latin open in front of me. I liked to study, but this time I couldn't concentrate. Fear and shame came to haunt me every time my uncle wrote from New York. The boys I knew, my classmates and the children of my grandparents' friends, all had very respectable fathers. According to my grandparents, mine was an unwashed, illiterate, violent man. When my friends asked me about my parents I told them they were both dead.

I daydreamed often that he wasn't my father at all. I dreamed that my real father had fought in the Civil War with my Uncle John and had been captured. One day he would get free and come live with us in London. Or my father was a member of royalty and had been held hostage by the woodsman. My mother had been forced to say that he was not her husband in order to save him. Someday my real father would kill the woodsman and take me and my grandparents to live with him in his castle. On days like this I just wished my uncle would write that my father was dead, so I wouldn't have to fear him anymore.

When my grandmother came to call me for dinner she chided me for not working on my studies. "You will never get into Harvard law school by sitting there daydreaming, William," she said.

"Oxford law school," I automatically corrected. "Grandmother, would my father have a legal right to come over here and take me? I mean if he did come to take me would you and grandfather have to let him?"

She stared at me for a moment with a look that seemed both horrified and bewildered. "I had no idea that you would worry about such a thing William. How long has this been on your mind?"

"All my life, I guess, at least, as long as I can remember. Isn't that why we came to England in the first place, so he couldn't get me?"

"Yes, it is the reason but it's only a precaution. For all we know he's forgotten about you. It may be that he's married again and has other children, but I think it most likely that it would be very inconvenient to fit a child into his lifestyle. I am sure he tried to get you just to be disagreeable to your grandfather and me. Oh dear, I wish I had known you were worrying about this all the time."

"But what if he still does want me?"

"I'm afraid I made my point too well. I thought you would know you were safe here. William, your father is too poor to get passage to England even if he wanted to, though I assure you it's not his sort of place."

"But what if someone loaned him the money?"

"I promise you, William, that your grandfather and I will never let your father take you. You are safe here, and I don't want you to worry about it a minute longer. Now come down to dinner."

I hoped she would remember this conversation the next time a letter came from Uncle John. I wished she would never speak of my father again.

My wish came true in a terrible way.

Less than two weeks after my conversation with Grandmother the headmaster of my school stopped me as I was leaving my last class. This was a shock for I assumed I'd done something wrong. He was a special friend of my grandparents, but that didn't decrease the awe and fear he inspired in me. If I was in trouble with him I would be in worse trouble at home.

But I wasn't in that kind of trouble. He told me

that I must not go home. No one was there. Hardwick would come later to pick me up. I was to wait in his office.

I waited and tried to study, but I felt very uneasy. The headmaster was obviously upset. Finally he pushed himself away from his desk and started pacing back and forth in front of me.

"I have something to tell you, William," he said. "I was going to leave this whole matter to Hardwick, but I think that would be a low thing to do considering the responsibility the poor man is burdened under already."

This statement frightened me, but I couldn't come up with any idea of what he might be talking about. After pacing three or four times across the room he turned to me and said, "Your grandparents have been in an accident, William. Their carriage was hit by a train. Apparently the horses went out of control and ran across the tracks."

It seemed like it took an hour for him to say the next thing.

"They have been taken to hospital. Now we can only wait for Hardwick to bring us more news."

I didn't want to wait. Even if the news was the worst I wanted to know then. I gave up my books and sat, thinking. Over and over I tried to picture the accident happening my way: my grandparents saw what was happening and jumped clear. When the carriage was hit it bounced off the train and was not shattered, they were not really in the carriage at all but had let someone else use it.

I listened for Hardwick to drive up and tried to resist the urge to look out the window. He came at last and walked into the room looking more tired and shaken than I would have thought a butler could look. He glanced at me, then at the headmaster, then at some spot on the far wall.

"Please sit down Hardwick," the headmaster said.

"I've told the boy all I know. You are free to tell us all you can. There is no easier way."

Hardwick looked at the headmaster. "Mr. Van Daam is still holding on, but Madam, I'm afraid, has left us. I am sorry, William." He said this not looking at me but at the floor. I remember thinking that "left us" was a strange way to put it.

Hardwick said my grandfather had been asking to see me and had muttered something about my father, what he must tell me about my father.

This was the first I'd thought about my father during all that time and I didn't stop to think about him long then. I had lost my grandmother, the only mother I had ever known.

I stayed that night at the headmaster's. By morning my grandfather had died. This was an even greater shock because I'd somehow convinced myself that I had had my share of bad fortune, that good was due me now as a sort of balance. For some time I was so full of mourning and confusion that I barely thought at all. I did what I was told and asked no questions of anyone.

Later, I thought of my father and wondered what my grandfather had wanted to tell me about him. Had it been a warning? I couldn't remember my grandfather ever speaking of him at all and once when I tried to ask a question about him Grandfather only said, "Now, none of that, you know how your grandmother feels."

Grandfather had never been chatty with me. He believed his job was to provide for our welfare. Domestic matters were left to women and servants. His answer hadn't surprised me, but it did surprise me that he would want to speak about my father on his death bed.

Uncle John came from New York to handle affairs, one of them being me. Hardwick, knowing how matters stood with my father, assumed I would be left in England, so he made arrangements for me to go to a reputable boys school not far from London. I thought this was a good thing as I would occasionally get to see Hardwick.

But my Uncle John came. I pictured him always as he looked in the photograph on the mantle, tall and slim and dressed in his uniform. He had been very somber looking, but that was only right for he was going off to war and any man fighting for a just cause should be serious about it. He was a splendid looking man and I was finally going to meet him.

When I saw him the first time it was at my home. Hardwick picked him up at the station and left him at the house then came to get me at the headmaster's where I was staying. Uncle John was sorting through papers in my grandfather's study when I went in. His face was recognizably the same though older. At last he was here, someone who knew and loved my grandparents too. I went up to him, put my arms around him and cried. He put his arm half around me and patted me on the shoulder. He was uncomfortable. I realized this as soon as I'd composed myself a bit and stepped back. He was also not at all the way I'd pictured him. Except for his face he looked more like my grandfather than the young man in the picture. He was portly and his stomach looked like it was about to pop his vest buttons. He seemed stern and not at all accustomed to talking with children.

"I know it's been hard for you," he said, "having all this happen to you at once and being left alone. When I've finished everything I need to do here I'll take you back to America where you belong, out of this musty old house and this musty old country."

I stepped back in shock and thought, "this is my house and my country, and they are not musty, either one of them."

Hardwick spoke from behind me. "It has been my understanding, sir, that the boy's father is a bit, ah, unsavory and the boy must be kept at a safe distance until he comes of age. I have made arrangements for William to go to a good school. Some of the boys he knows will be going there next year, so there will be someone familiar..."

"Thank you Hardwick," my uncle broke in, "I'm confident that you have done your best according to your knowledge. William needs to be with his family. As for his father, you needn't fear any harm from that quarter."

I wanted to protest, but I knew better. This was one of those many matters I would have no say in. Uncle John was my guardian now. But America, I had forgotten to even worry about that. And what did he mean about my father? Was he dead?

"William," my uncle said, "Perhaps you and Hardwick should begin packing the things you want to take with you.

The two of us headed obediently toward the stairs but in the parlor I stopped and reached up to take the photograph of my mother. Hardwick's eyebrows lifted slightly as I looked at the one of my uncle.

"I suppose I should take it, shouldn't I? If he came in and saw that I had left it his feelings might be hurt."

"It's quite possible," Hardwick said, "and you might regret it later if you left it. You might become very fond of him. Perhaps one day you will even be glad that he took you back to America." But I thought he sounded doubtful.

"Never," I said."I have always been an Englishman at heart and I will come back somehow. Maybe a miracle will happen and I'll be able to convince him to send me back here for school."

I took down the photo of my uncle, and we went on up the stairs. At the top I paused at the first door, my grandparents' room. "Do you think it would be improper for me to take something out of their room," I asked, "something to remember them by?"

"I think, under the circumstances, it would be quite

acceptable."

I went in feeling very much like an intruder. I was uncomfortable and took the first thing that caught my eye; a photograph of my grandparents together, taken several years before.

We went on into my room, and I sat on the bed while Hardwick packed my things. I wanted to take my bed and my desk, but he said I would only be allowed those things I could fit into trunks. I would miss my desk though it was now becoming a bit too small for me. I had done my studies on it for years. I was allowed to take my books. I loved them, and it would have been a terrible loss to leave them.

Two days later I said good-bye to Hardwick and made him promise he would write to me. I said goodbye to London, too, as our ship sailed down the Thames. It was June, early morning and there was a fog. I was sure I would be coming back soon.

CHAPTER TWO

Crossing the Atlantic was much like crossing the channel only longer and more tedious. I'm ashamed to say I got bored. My uncle seemed to hold to the common belief that children should be seen and not heard and should speak only when spoken to. My grandfather had been this way with me, and I was comfortable with it.

I shared a cabin with my uncle, but I learned almost nothing about him. The one thing I did learn was that he could not be trusted.

I finally got up the nerve to ask him if my father had died.

"No, he hasn't died."

That was all he said at the time. Later, at dinner, he asked, "Are you looking forward to seeing your father?"

"No." I said.

I was curious and would have liked to see him maybe from a distance, if I knew I wouldn't have to have any dealings with him. But my uncle hadn't asked me that.

He scowled. "He's looking forward to seeing you."

"I don't want to see him."

He cleared his throat then stared at me for a while with a strange look on his face. Finally he said, "I think you ought to know that you probably can't believe everything my mother told you about your father. Of course I don't know what she said, but experience tells me that it was exaggerated and far too harsh."

"How dare you accuse my grandmother of lying." I said as I jumped up from my chair. I ran back to our cabin and wondered how I could stand to be with him any longer. If I'd known before we left England what my uncle had planned for me I would have made an effort to escape him while I was still there. Now I knew that running away was my only way to escape and get back home. I would never convince him to send me back. But I had no money. Somehow I would have to find a job.

I waited in great agitation for my uncle to return from his meal. I was hungry, having had my outburst before our food came, and worried about what he would do to me for speaking so rudely to him. I considered hiding somewhere in the ship and not coming out until we got to New York. I would get even hungrier. I might even die before we got there. Even worse, I would never see my books again.

My uncle was gruff but didn't mention my outburst, nor did he mention any change in his plans for me.

I was with my uncle's family only a week, which was just as well. My Aunt Hope was quiet and paid almost no attention to me. My four cousins were tiresome. The baby cried most of the time and the oldest, Amanda, who was eight, kept telling me how happy I should be in America because America was the very best place to live. The middle two, Jack and Flora, followed me around and stared. I couldn't find a quiet place to be alone and read or think.

My uncle told me the day after we landed that the travel arrangements had already been made for my trip into the northern mountains. I was being taken to live with my father.

I spent most of my time that week plotting out my course of action and decided I needed to escape somewhere between the city and the place where my father lived. It must be far enough from New York City to be unfamiliar to my uncle and a safe distance from my father as well. I would leave the train when it made a short stop at some small town and if I was lucky the train would be on its way again before my uncle realized I had gotten off. I would search the countryside for a farmer who needed help. From my little experience I assumed all farmers needed laborers at one time or another. Once I found a place where I would be fed I could look around for something better.

My uncle took me shopping for a few essentials, being: one stout pair of walking shoes, one pair of winter boots, two pair of woolen long johns, one wool shirt, one cotton shirt, two pair of wool pants (cotton pants I had already, but my wool ones I had outgrown), mittens, a hat, and several pairs of socks. I had a heavy coat that I brought with me from England. I was also given a leather shoulder bag and told I could carry any personal items I could fit in it. My clothes and this small bag were all I was allowed to take. I put my mother's photo, my grandparents' photo and my copy of <u>David Copperfield</u> in the bag. This was the only book I was allowed to take. I wondered why he let me bring all my things to America only to have to leave them behind in the end.

I decided my uncle wanted them for himself. Probably he had other reasons for bringing me over, too. It must have been for money. Perhaps my grandparents left me their money and my uncle wanted it. If he sent me into the woods to be lost and possibly to die then he would get the money without any fuss. Why else would he have dragged me over here when he could have left me in England and not been bothered with me.

It was hard for me to leave my things in the city. I was sure my little cousins would destroy them in weeks, and even if I was able to reclaim them there would be nothing left. It was harder still when I realized that we weren't traveling by train but by boat up the Hudson River. I would have to revise my plan. I certainly couldn't leave a steamer in mid-stream.

We traveled up river all night, but early the next morning the boat docked in Albany and we boarded a train.We had already come 140 miles.

Now I had a chance to carry out my plan. We were going through farm land and small towns but even more of the landscape was wooded. At times the train passed through miles of woods at a time and it looked like we were traveling in a green tunnel. I began to wonder if this was the sort of place it would be wise to try my fortunes in. The stretches of wood became longer and I decided I must try soon. But I added one more thing to my plan. A gun. Somehow I had to get a gun. These woods must be filled with dangerous wild animals and Indians. In every story I had ever read about America the men all carried guns. It was very exciting to read about but not so appealing when I was right in the middle of it all. So far I did not like America.

We changed from the Delaware and Hudson to the Adirondack Railroad in a town named Saratoga. My uncle didn't let me out of his sight. As we were changing trains we happened to meet a man my uncle knew, a business acquaintance. His name was Grayson, and he was traveling with his wife and daughter. We sat with them.

Mr. Grayson was a pleasant man, good humored and ready to talk about any subject my uncle introduced. The two women were both sharp tongued and the daughter talked too much and tried to enter into the men's conversation. She was not a child, old enough to be married at least. Probably no one wants her, I thought, because she doesn't know her place. Maybe this was the way things were done in America, but in England the women didn't try to take part in the men's serious conversations.

The train stopped at a small town and I told my uncle I wanted to get up and look around. He said I wasn't to leave my seat unless the train was in motion. So that was that. My only hope was to devise another plan.

The fields we passed were mostly ragged around the edges like the wild parts were trying to take back the land. The English landscape was neat and orderly. I felt very homesick.

I had long since stopped listening to the adults'

conversation, so I was surprised when my uncle turned to me and said, "William, I've decided that when the railroad ends I'll go back and have you finish your journey with the Graysons. They've volunteered, and I'm pleased to avoid the stage trip." He turned to Mr. Grayson and said, "William's father refuses to ride the stage. He claims it's bad for the health." He smiled. It was the first time I'd seen him do that. It changed the way he looked.

What sort of man wouldn't even ride in a stage? It seemed my father must be even more backward than I'd thought.

I felt even more strongly that I had to escape. With my uncle gone it should be easier.

In North Creek we went straight from the train to the stage. My uncle spoke to the driver, who was loading the bags. It wasn't a proper stage with doors but an open, three seated buckboard with a canvas roof. **H. Bradley** was printed on the part of the canvas that hung down.

Uncle John came over and shook Mr. Grayson's hand. "Charles, I can't tell you how much I appreciate this," he said. "I can only hope for your sakes that the mud has dried up. William, I hope you will not disgrace your grandparents' upbringing by using bad manners. Obey the Graysons. They'll take care of you for the duration of the trip." Then he shook the driver's hand and said "Good luck to you, Mr. Bradley". He turned and boarded the train.

I soon began to like the Graysons, and I wished I didn't have to think of them as my jailers. All three of them showed an interest in me and included me in their conversation. I wasn't used to this from adults.

"Your Uncle says you're in America for the first time," Mr. Grayson said.

"I was born here, but I don't remember anything."

"And how do you like our vast wilderness?" he

said. "You know, in England you have certain separate woods here and there surrounded by fields and towns. But here in America it's one continuous forest with the towns and farms carved out of them. The woods always seem to try their best to take back what was theirs." He said this as though he was proud of it, and I thought that a very strange thing. But he had spoken of England as though it were mine, and I warmed to him because of that.

"Have you been to England?" I asked.

"We were there last year for a month, and we all loved it even though Papa might not want to admit it," Elizabeth Grayson said.

"Of course I'll admit it, it is a very nice place, very pretty and educational and all, but there's no place like home, is there?"He gave me a look that seemed to say that he knew how homesick I was.

"Did you go to London?" I asked. "That's where my home is."

"Yes of course we went to London. We visited the museums, Westminster Abbey, St. Paul's Cathedral and Buckingham Palace. We went to the theater and fit just as many things as we could into our week there. It's a wonderful city."

I grinned and could feel myself flushing with pride. I wanted to tell them that I would be going back soon. I wished I could tell them about my father and my plan and ask for their help, but I knew they would never believe my Uncle John could be doing something that bad. And I didn't want them to think badly of me. The Graysons were such kindly people and higher class than most I'd met since coming here. They were people my grandparents would have approved of.

Before long I discovered why my Uncle had stayed behind regardless of good companions. The road was rough and awful and the four of us bounced around on the seats. Because of my light weight it seemed that I was hardly ever in contact with the seat. I was next to Mrs. Grayson, and I kept being thrown against her. Mr. Grayson seemed very pleased. He kept saying, "Isn't this terrible, Nellie. Isn't this just as bad as I told you it would be? There's worse yet to come, though. The stretch between Indian Lake and Blue Mountain Lake is rockier. You'll see." "If it gets any worse than this I may just get out and walk." She grumbled.

I was getting hungry, and I wondered how I would feed myself if I escaped.

Mr. Grayson must have been hungry himself because he turned to me and said, "We only have another mile or so before we stop to eat."

"Do you really expect me to eat and get back in this thing?" His wife said. "No human alive could keep their food down with all this bouncing."

Nevertheless, when we stopped at the North River Hotel we all ate and none of us lost any of it later.

I looked for my chance to escape at this stop, but the stage driver kept his eye on me and even followed me to the privy. I was becoming desperately afraid that I would have to meet my father. We were so deep into the woods now that I felt I would be in terrible danger if I tried to go off on my own. I had to rework my plan, but I had run out of ideas.

After a long and rough ride we went through Indian Lake.This town had a few hotels and cleared land, but there was only one road and most of the view was simply woods in all directions.

"Mr. Grayson, where do people buy things they need, things like food and knives." I asked this cautiously and didn't mention guns.

"Some of the hotels have stores in them. Some buy what they need with money, but most of the people around here trade furs, meat and farm goods for what they need."

After we passed through the town we crossed a

river and stopped at Jackson's Arctic Hotel.

"This is our last stop, William, our dinner stop." Mr. Grayson said. "I don't know about you, but that rough ride didn't do anything to curb my appetite."

I hung back as Mr. Bradley went up the stairs. He stopped to talk to two men who were sitting on the porch. One was older, maybe the age of my uncle, and wore a long thick moustache. The other man was young looking, like a university student. His hair was blonde and straight and parted in the middle. He wore no moustache. A small brown and black dog lay at his feet. This second man looked vaguely familiar, perhaps like someone I'd known casually in London. Mr. Bradley called out to the Graysons, "You folks better come on in and get your meal." They went up the stairs, chatting with one another and left me alone.

I couldn't believe it. I had my chance to get away. I wasn't sure what to do. The older man on the porch went inside. The blonde one looked straight down at me and said, "How was the ride?" He was grinning very wide, and I supposed he knew all about the ride, so I just groaned and rolled my eyes. I was surprised he took notice of me.

He said, "If you think that was bad wait till you hit the rest of it. The last stretch is the worst by far." He grinned again.

I knew this would be my only chance, so I blurted out, "I don't plan to go any farther; I want to find a job. Do you know anyone here who needs a boy to help them, a farmer, maybe, or a widow lady?" I was closer to him now and could see that he was not as young as I thought at first.

"Well, I don't know of any widow ladies off hand, and all the farmers in these parts seem to have plenty of kids of their own to help out." He looked thoughtful for a minute. "Are you sure you want to do this? It seems mighty strange a boy your age making that trip up here just to look for a job. Don't you have any folks?"

I was desperate, so I decided to risk that he would help me if he knew the trouble I was in. I spoke fast because I was afraid that any moment the driver would remember he wasn't supposed to leave me alone and come out to get me.

"I was orphaned when my grandparents died and my uncle has sent me here to the woods in exile, so he can get my inheritance. I'm all alone and have no money and nowhere to go." I lied just a little because I was afraid he might know my father or at least have heard of him and he might feel it his duty to make me go on.

He looked at me thoughtfully and rubbed his chin. "Now that is a sorry state of affairs," he said. "Well, I'm not a farmer, I'm a trapper and guide, and I've been working alone, but I could use some help. I can't pay much, but I'll provide food and a bed free. You ever do any trapping or is all your experience in farming?"

"To tell the truth, I've been a schoolboy all my life," I said. But if you'll still take me, can we go now please?"

"Right," he said, "You got any bags on the stage?"

"Just that one bag right there." I pointed it out to him and he took it down and carried it to the corner of the building. He jumped up onto the porch, climbed over the railing and handed down a big basket. It was made of strips of wood woven together and had leather straps on it. The man jumped to the ground and swung the basket up to his back. When he got his arms through the straps both hands were free, and he picked up my bag in his right hand and started off towards the woods.The little dog jumped off after him and I followed, holding my leather satchel against my side. I hurried to keep up with them, turning around often to see if anyone was following us. After only a few minutes I couldn't see the hotel or the road.

"You sound to me like you're from England," he said without turning around.

"Yes, I grew up in London." Then the thought suddenly came to me that when he found out how useless I was going to be to him he might get mad and leave me on my own. I decided I had better make a clean breast of it before we got too far into the woods. "To tell you the truth Sir, I don't know anything at all about trapping, and I don't even know what guiding is. I'm afraid I might not be much help".

"Look here," he said, and he turned around and grinned wide at me. "I can't have you calling me sir, we're almost partners. Besides, I don't like anybody to be that formal with me." He held out his hand for me to shake, and when I reached for it he said, "My name is Benson Chadwick. You can call me Ben or Pa, whichever you prefer. Do you mind if I call you Will?"

CHAPTER THREE

So many things went through my head that I don't know how long I stood there with him grasping my hand and grinning at me. Finally I said, "You can't be my father, you're too young."

I snatched my hand away and stepped back, furious at him for tricking me, then laughing at me. And of all the stupid things I could have said that was the stupidest. Of course he was my father. He looked like me, that's why he looked familiar. And he knew my name. That was why the stage driver didn't watch after me anymore.

"Does that driver know your name?"

"Of course, everyone knows everyone else around here. He knew you were coming a month ago."

"I didn't get my dinner," I said. I looked back the way we came but I couldn't see any trace of a path.

"You aren't thinking of going back to get it are you?" I shook my head and felt helpless and trapped.

"I had the cook wrap up some food to take with us." He put down his pack, reached way down inside it and brought out a bundle wrapped in brown paper. "If you're really hungry we can eat right here, but I had a better spot in mind if you can wait."

"I'm not hungry," I said. The last thing I wanted to do was eat. I felt all stirred up inside. This was the man I had feared all my life, and he seemed so friendly. What kind of trick was he playing on me? He looked clean and smart. Why had my grandparents hated him?

"I can wait," I said.

I swatted my face. The mosquitoes were gathering. My father put the food back, fished out a little bottle and held it up for me to see. "I didn't put any of this on before. I didn't want to scare you off with the smell, but now that the introductions are over I think we should dispense with formalities for the sake of comfort." He poured a little of the stuff into his hand and smeared it on his face and neck and the backs of his hands. He handed me the bottle. "It's the only thing that keeps the bugs off."

It smelled like very bad medicine, and it stung the inside of my nose when I drew breath, but it did keep the mosquitoes away.

"Works doesn't it?" my father said then he swung the pack onto his back and started walking.

As I followed, I wondered what my life was going to be like with him and how I was going to escape. What if I decided I liked my father? But thinking that gave me a terrible pang of guilt at the disloyalty I was showing for my grandparents. Hadn't they looked after me all those years? Hadn't they planned all the best things for me? If I stayed here I would never get the education I needed to become a lawyer. Besides, there must be a good reason why they hated my father. I decided I must be on my guard and not trust him too much.

I knew that I should keep track of where we were going so I could find my way back out. But it was useless to try. The woods are so dense, I thought, that even if I do manage to get a gun I will be too lost to use it.

It was then that I realized my father wasn't carrying a gun. I wondered if he was friendly with the Indians. I began to hear little sounds I hadn't noticed before and kept craning my neck around to see what was behind me. I remembered that the books I had read said that Indians could move without making a sound and ordinary people couldn't see them unless they chose to be seen.

I wanted to ask my father something and realized that to get his attention I would have to make a decision about what to call him. My very strict upbringing made it impossible for me to call him by his first name. I couldn't call him Mr. Chadwick, and I didn't want to call him Pa because that is what he wanted me to do. I decided on Dad. I tried it out.

"Dad."

"Yes," he said, giving me a look over his shoulder but not stopping.

"Why don't you have a gun?"

"Oh I have one. I just didn't bring it with me."

"Why not?"

"I wasn't sure how much you would have. I might not have been able to carry it. Why?"

"I just thought it might be kind of dangerous to be walking through the woods without a gun. I mean, well, are you friendly with the Indians?"

He stopped by a fallen log, put down my bag and slid his pack to the ground. He was grinning again. "There aren't any Indians around here, at least right now." He sat down with his back against the log. "I think it's time for a short rest. Why don't you sit down." The dog flopped down and laid his head across my father's knee. "I don't think you and Sammy have been introduced. This is my faithful little dog. He may not be very friendly at first. Sammy doesn't like competition, but he'll get used to you."

I sat down next to my father but not too close. Sammy ignored me, which was fine. I hadn't been around dogs and didn't have much interest in them.

I was thankful for the rest. I had to work hard to keep up with my father, and I was tired. "How far is it to Blue Mountain Lake?" I asked.

"Oh about twelve or thirteen miles as the crow flies."

"How far have we gone?"

"About three miles."

I groaned before I thought. I didn't want him to think I was weak, but I couldn't believe he was going to make me walk that far in one day and I didn't see how we could make it. It had been past four o'clock when we left the hotel, I was almost sure of it. "Are we going to walk through the night then?" I asked, trying to sound unconcerned.

"Oh no, we've just got a little over a mile to go tonight then we'll get an early start in the morning."

We set off again and walked till we came to a small body of water my father called Rock Lake. He led me a short way along the shore to a strange little building that was all open on one side and faced the lake. He called it a lean-to. The floor was elevated about a foot from the ground and he sat down on it to rustle around in what he kept calling his packbasket. First he pulled out the bundle of food and set it beside him then he handed me a small tin box. "Soap," he said. I always wash before I eat. You first."For a moment I just stood there holding the soap, not quite sure what to do with it. Then he pointed and said, "the lake". He followed me to the water, squatted beside me and we both washed our hands.

The smell of the bug repellent clung to me in spite of the strong soap, but I was far too hungry for it to bother my appetite. In the parcel there were two large slices of fried meat my father said was venison, four baked potatoes and a large piece of sweet corn bread.

"I'm afraid I didn't bring my cooking pans," my father said. "But if you're as hungry as I am you wouldn't want to wait anyway." He gave some of the food to the dog, but there was still plenty left to save for our breakfast.

It was getting darker and my father pulled two blankets out of his packbasket and gave one to me. "It's a warm night," he said. "We'll just roll up in these, nothing fancy. If you get cold let me know. Now, since it's a little early to be going to sleep why don't you tell me what you're carrying in that satchel you guard so carefully."

I had, for the whole walk, kept my leather bag clamped tightly beneath my arm and hadn't set it down even to wash my hands. "A book," I said, hoping he would lose interest. I didn't want to tell him about the pictures.

"What's the name of the book?"

"<u>David Copperfield</u>."

"So you're a fan of Dickens. Can I see it?"

I desperately tried to think of a reason not to hand it to him, but I couldn't come up with anything, so I took it out slowly. "You won't do anything to it will you?"

"Do anything? Why would I do anything to it?"

"Well, I thought you didn't want me to have books. I have so many and Uncle John would only let me carry what I could fit into this bag. I thought maybe you disapproved of books." I could hear my voice dwindling off as I tried to explain. Everything I said sounded stupid.

"Of course I don't disapprove of books. You act just like your mother. She was always concerned for the safety of her books before any other possession, even her clothes."

I stared at him in disbelief and wondered if he was my father after all and if he had really been married to my mother. I'd never heard that she cared a thing for reading or learning. She loved parties and dressing up for balls and flirting with handsome men with rich estates in the country. That was always how my grandmother had spoken of her.

My father reached over and took the book from me. "I haven't read this one yet. As a matter of fact the only Dickens I've read is <u>A Tale of Two Cities.</u>"

"You can read!" I was so surprised that I said it before I thought and was immediately embarrassed.

He sat there and stared at me for a moment with a very strange look on his face, then he said, "What on earth has that old battleaxe been telling you about me all these years? You never got my letters did you."

"You wrote me letters?"

"Starting when you were five and I figured you were learning to read. I sent them to John and he mailed them with his letters to his mother and father."

It seemed strange to hear them called John's mother and father like they had nothing to do with me, like they hadn't raised me all these years. "I didn't get any letters," I said, but I thought of how my grandmother was always angry when she got a letter from Uncle John.

"Grandmother always told me you would do this if you got the chance."

"Do what?"

"She said you would take me into the woods where there was no civilization and no schools. She said I would either die like my mother or grow up like an animal."

"Your grandmother and I had vastly different definitions of the word civilization. But you really thought I couldn't read? Your mother would never have married someone who couldn't read. What an outlandish idea!"

He handed the book back to me, and we sat for a while in silence. I was relieved that he didn't seem to be mad at me. I was also surprised that he kept mentioning my mother. I guess I thought he would be too ashamed of what he did to her to talk about her. When I stopped to think about it I remembered that my grandmother never actually said my father couldn't read. I had come to that conclusion on my own. But she had said that he was responsible for my mother's death.

The lean-to floor was hard, but I was warm enough, and I slept well. The dog slept curled up against my father's hip on the side away from me.

When I woke in the morning a thick fog lay over everything and only the ghostly shapes of the closest trees were visible. I was having to get used to relieving myself in the woods as there were no privies. I didn't like it. I didn't like going into the woods by myself because I could imagine strange things coming out of the trees and attacking me. This morning the fog made it even worse. I went around behind the lean-to, keeping the corner of it always in sight.

When I came back my father handed me the soap and told me to wash my hands and face before breakfast. "If you want to stay healthy," he said, "always wash your hands before you eat and after you relieve yourself. As many people die from filth as anything else. Filth and spoiled food that is. Spoiled food gets a lot. Don't forget that."

As I ate I wondered what kind of crazy man he was. I wanted to like him, but I also wanted to believe my grandmother. I felt I was betraying her if I trusted my father. I was confused and wished Hardwick were there. He would be able to figure out the situation I was in and help me understand what to do. Maybe he was worrying about what was happening to me. I decided I would send a letter to him the first chance I got.

My father folded and packed our blankets, and we started out with the fog still thick. He said it would thin out as soon as we climbed a bit and he was right. Soon after leaving the fog we came to a long stretch where most of the trees had been cut down, leaving stumps and underbrush.

"The loggers have been through here," my father said. "They cut near the water first. It's easier to get the logs out that way. They float them down the rivers in the spring when the water is high."

The walking seemed much easier than the day before, so much of the way was cleared and there was very little climbing. Most of the time I could see patches of fog below us to the right. It was lying on the river my father said.

After maybe two hours we came upon a road. "That's where the stage came through last night," he said.

We followed the road until we crossed the river on a short bridge then we left it again. I was wishing we could have stayed on it and wondering how much longer we would have to walk when we came to the shore of a lake. It was much bigger than Rock lake. A huge mountain rose up from the shore across the water. "Blue Mountain and Blue Mountain Lake," my father said.

"It seems an awfully big mountain."

"I've heard there are mountains in the west that are three or four times higher than that, but for the two of us I guess this is big enough. We may be at the top of that mountain before the day is over."

We went to the edge of the lake, and he lifted a small boat out from under some trees.He put it half in the water and half out then began loading our things. I was amazed at his strength. I say the boat was small, but it was not so small that I would have thought a man capable of picking it up. Both ends were pointed. Toward the middle it widened considerably and the edges rode low to the water. Two oars were tucked under the seats. The boat was a little over twice as long as my father was tall.

When he'd set our things in the bow he slid the whole thing into the water, so it was floating. He motioned to the side of me. "Step onto that rock and from there you can get into the stern seat." I got in and the thing rocked terribly. I was sure I would tip it over before I could sit down. Once I was sitting it seemed that even the slightest moves I made, even a deep breath, sent me rocking. I was terrified. My father said "Sammy", and the dog jumped onto the rock I'd been standing on then into the boat. He settled himself down next to my father's packbasket. My father pointed the boat toward the middle of the lake then shoved off and jumped on in one movement. I clung to the sides for dear life. I couldn't swim.

He sat down facing me then pulled out the oars and fixed them to the boat. I saw that there was a short paddle under the seats as well. He let the oars hang in the water. "Before we go anywhere I'm going to give you a short lesson on guideboats," he said. "You're in the stern, Sammy is in the bow, and I am amidships. These are the oars and these are the oarlocks. What the oarlocks are fitted into are the oarlock sockets. You can see there are two sets of oarlock sockets because sometimes I row from the middle seat and sometimes from the bow seat. The paddle down there is for using on narrow rivers when the oars are too long. The person in the stern seat paddles."

I fervently hoped we were not going down any narrow rivers that day.

"When you row you can't pull your hands back at the same time because the oars overlap. You have to pull them back one after the other, like this. It takes a little getting used to at first. You can't see where you're going so you have to peek behind yourself now and then, and find yourself a landmark astern to row straight away from. You'll see better when you try it yourself."

Surely he wouldn't expect me to row the thing. I could barely keep from tipping it over just trying to sit still.

"Now here is the most important thing. This boat must be treated like your most priceless possession. Never scrape it along things. Lift it up and set it down gently when you're putting it in or out of the water, and never get in the boat when it's on shore. Our lives can easily depend on this boat. Our living definitely depends on this boat. No boat, no money." He was acting more stern than I had seen him. For the first time he actually sounded like a father.

He'd said I must lift the boat when putting it into the water. I wondered how he expected me to do that. "How much does it weigh?" I asked.

"About sixty-five, seventy pounds."

"But I weigh more than that."

"Oh yes, it's a very light boat, it has to be because I carry it from lake to lake on my shoulders, and I have to carry my packbasket too."

He grabbed the oars and with a couple of pulls had us headed across the lake. We were going much faster than I'd expected. Behind us, not far from where we'd been, was a hotel. I swiveled my head around, trying to move my body as little as possible, and saw another hotel vaguely in the direction we were going. "All I see are hotels, doesn't anybody just live here?"

"Not many, not yet anyway. Some of the hotel owners stay through the winter. Let's see, on Raquette Lake there are eight besides me and three new men starting to build. That's twelve altogether. Five of them take in visitors.The other fellows are just building themselves summer homes. But Raquette's a big lake, and we don't get in each other's way much. We meet more here at Blue or up in Long Lake because they've got the stage, and our clients come in there.

"So you don't live here? You live on that other lake?"

"That's right.We're here to pick up the Grayson family, three people. Tomorrow we'll be off where ever they want to go. That's why I picked you up at Jackson's hotel, I thought we should get to know one another a bit before we had a bunch of people around us."

I couldn't help but smile. The Graysons, I'd be seeing them again. "I rode on the stage with them," I said. "I like them."

"Good. You see, this is why you couldn't bring your books with you right now. I have to worry about ferrying passengers around. I don't have room for extra baggage. John will send them up this winter and we'll pull them over the ice."

This was great. I would see the Graysons, and I would get my books. Two pieces of good news at once. But of course I wasn't planning to stay until winter. Then I had another thought. "Are you going to put all three of the Graysons in this boat?"

"Oh no, Charlie Blanchard will be there. You and I

will take one of them, and Charlie will take the other two."

We were at the other side now. The bow of the boat made a little crunching sound as it hit the sand. Sammy jumped out then my father climbed out over the bow and lifted the baggage out. I came next then he lifted the boat up onto the sand and tipped it over with the oars back up under the seats. He put my case under there too and took his packbasket.

A little path lead from the beach into the woods. Almost as soon as we started along it we began to climb. This was a clear, well used path, but it was very steep, and I couldn't keep up.

My father stopped. "You go first and set the pace, so I won't lose you. You'll get used to the exercise in no time," he said. I moved around him and took the lead.

Finally we came out into a level clearing with a small hotel and its outbuildings. The Graysons were sitting on the porch.

"William, how good it is to see you again so soon." Mr. Grayson stood up to greet me and shake my hand. "Is this your father?"

I made introductions all around and felt very grown up.

"We're a little late," my father said, "But we got the right day, the seventh day of the seventh month of eighteen seventy seven. They say seven is a lucky number. If it is then this should be one lucky day." My father looked at me as he finished speaking and winked. I realized it was my birthday. I was ten.

"Hey, Ben, you finally made it." A stranger came around the corner of the building and slapped my father on the back. "I was beginning to think we'd have to go on without you."

"Now none of that, Charlie. We've still got a good two hours of morning left. I didn't think these good people would be ready to get out much earlier than this after that stage ride yesterday."

Mr. Grayson laughed and Mrs. Grayson grumbled something about being dragged into uncivilized places. But Elizabeth lifted her chin and said, "I'll have you know that we are made of sterner stuff than that, Mr. Chadwick. Just because we're from the city doesn't mean we have to be coddled."

"Well now, since I was a city boy myself once I'll have to agree with you. And, since I didn't ride the stage and won't ride the stage, at least through that part of the country, you must certainly be made of sterner stuff than I." He said it with one of his grins.

She grinned back. "So where are you and Charlie going to take us, Mr. Chadwick?"

"Ben, everybody calls me Ben, Miss Grayson."

She laughed. "All right then, my name is Elizabeth. Please don't forget it."

"Mr. Grayson thought he'd like to climb to the top of the mountain if you think the ladies can manage it," Charlie said.

"I wouldn't dare suggest they couldn't. I'll go inside and see if they can put us up a lunch. It'll be a good way to show Will his new home, though the view from here isn't bad."

I hadn't looked behind me since we broke out into the open. I turned and saw the lake below me and a chain of lakes beyond it curving gradually to the right until the haze obscured the view. All around us the mountains rose randomly.

I had to admit to myself that if I were on holiday with my grandparents and saw such a sight I would have thought it grand and beautiful. If I were with a group of my school friends I would have even looked forward to a bit of outdoor living. But I was expected to stay here for good and sleep outside on a regular basis and climb up and down these endless mountains. I felt trapped.

My father came out with the lunch, packed it, and we were off to climb the mountain. I hadn't had much of a rest. Fortunately for me the women's skirts were a problem as they kept catching on branches. This slowed us down and gave me a chance to get my breath now and then. This trail went relentlessly uphill. I was hungry by the time we reached the top but apparently my father was too because he said, "Let's have our little picnic before we do our sightseeing if you all don't mind. Will and I had our breakfast very early this morning."

"I, for one, am quite ready to sit down," Mrs. Grayson said.

"This is a fine job you men have," Mr. Grayson said after we'd settled for our meal. "Oh, I realize you probably get sick of ramming through the woods in all kinds of weather for very small pay. But you have no idea how much I would like to trade places with you sometimes."

"I can't speak for Charlie," my father said, "but I certainly do have an idea. I'm here doing this job because I felt the same way.After ten years I haven't changed my mind."

"I was a teacher before I moved here," Charlie said. "I can't say the pay is any better or any worse, but I wouldn't go back to it. Too much freedom here. Hard to do something else after you've been your own boss."

"Well, I'm a teacher right now," Elizabeth said, "and I can tell you, the pay is not good. I make barely enough to pay for my little room and my board."

"So you don't live with your parents?" My father asked.

"No, I teach in Schenectady. I couldn't get a position in Albany. Maybe next year."

I was surprised and a bit shocked that such a good family would allow such a thing. My Grandmother believed it was 'common' for a woman to support herself if she had any male relative who could support her. Elizabeth became a curiosity to me because of this. I wondered if anyone would ever want to marry her.

When we finished eating my father took me aside. He pointed out Blue Mountain Lake and the series of lakes that curved out beyond it. It was clear from here that much of it was one big lake. "That's Raquette," my father said.

The top of the mountain had been completely cleared of trees and we could see water glinting here and there in all directions. He started pointing and naming. Mountains, rivers, lakes and ponds. I couldn't even tell which ones he was pointing at. Charlie came up to us and laughed. "You don't expect the boy to remember any of that do you? He hasn't even seen these places on the ground yet."

My father dropped his hand. "I guess you're right. I'll bring him back in a couple of years."

He sounded disappointed and I thought maybe I should show interest in something, so I asked why the trees were all cut down up here so far from water. This seemed to cheer him up. "Surveying," he said. "I came up here four years ago with Verplanck Colvin, the State surveyor, along with a few other fellows. I came back again with him last summer to finish the job. He had to have a clear view in all directions to be able to use his instruments. We built those two shacks over there to sleep in and keep the instruments out of the rain."

By now Mr. Grayson had come over to listen in on the conversation. He had questions about the surveying, the height of the mountains and the names of the lakes. I left them alone and wandered over to look at the shacks.

After a while I saw Mrs. Grayson and Elizabeth start back down the mountain. I went with them. It was a great relief to be going down-hill for a change.

We were almost to the hotel when the men caught up with us. As far as I could figure, they were talking about the medicinal value of plants.

Once back the adults settled on the porch, and I wandered behind the barn to watch the animals. There were chickens, a cow, two horses and some sheep back there.

My father called me to come and eat, and when I got there he handed me a bowl of water. I was embarrassed that he did it in front of everybody and wondered if I looked as dirty as all that. But Charlie laughed and said, "I guess I'm next in line for the wash.We call your father 'wash basin Ben' around here. Have to get used to it boy, he's a regular tyrant about it.

"An excellent habit," Mrs. Grayson said. "I'm thankful my husband picked such a careful man for our guide."

It was the first positive thing I heard her say. But from that time she favored him and never had a bad word to say about him.

We had mutton for dinner. It was very good and reminded me of home. After the meal the cook brought out a long, flat cake with one very large candle burning in the middle of it. Everyone clapped and cried "Happy Birthday Will" and told me to blow out my candle. I was astonished.

It must have shown on my face because my father laughed and said, "Didn't you know it was your birthday?"

"Well, yes," I said, "but how did you know?"

"I was there wasn't I? I'm a bit absent minded at times, but I'm not that bad. Here now, just a minute, I've got something for you." He jumped up from the table and went into the next room. He came back with a new looking gun and laid it on my lap. "I don't know if a boy brought up in London has any hankering for a gun like boys brought up here, but you'll be needing it anyway, and I figured it was as good a gift as any."

I stared at it. I'd been scheming about how to secretly get a gun then suddenly there was one dropped into my lap. I said, "Yes, I have been wanting a gun, but I don't know how to use it."

"Oh, that's all right." My father beamed his young smile at me. "I've got all summer to teach you."

CHAPTER FOUR

I was stiff and sore the next morning, so sore that I could barely walk. My father rubbed my legs and told me the best thing I could do was get out and walk off the stiffness. I thought it was a mean joke, but I discovered he was right. If I kept moving, after a while my legs wouldn't be too bad, but the longer I stayed in one spot the worse they felt when I started out again.

"It's too bad we can't go out and walk another ten miles," my father said as we were getting ready to leave. "But boating is what's on the schedule for today. We have to get the Graysons out on the lakes fishing and sightseeing. That's what they're paying us for."

The walk down to the beach was the most exercise I got that day and the inside of the guideboat was not the best place to stretch my legs. I was put in the bow seat this time because I was a lot lighter than Mr. Grayson who was in the stern. The luggage was arranged near my feet and Sammy lay just the other side of it. My father said it was best if the boat sat fairly level in the water with the bow just slightly higher. The way he fixed things that was how it was. I faced where we had been this time and my father's back as well. It didn't much matter where I faced since none of it was familiar to me anyway. Most of the time I watched the mountain as it got smaller and smaller behind us.

We soon crossed Blue Mountain Lake and went through a short passage to Eagle Lake. My father aimed us in the right direction, gave a sharp pull on the oars and we were through. Charlie was a comfortable distance behind us with the ladies. Eagle Lake was small and soon we were into a narrow channel leading to another lake, Utowana. Mr. Grayson paddled us through. I looked around my father's back to see Mrs. Grayson holding the paddle in Charlie's boat. Her back was stiff and she had a stern look of concentration on her face.

They didn't run into anything. I thought maybe I could do it if I tried. I was getting used to the feeling of the boat. It didn't seem as tippy as it had at first.

Utowana was a little bigger than Eagle Lake but it wasn't long before my father slowed us down and slid my end of the boat gently into the shore. I was surprised. I didn't know we were even close to the end of the lake. Though he looked back when he moved us to shore he slowed down first. "How could you tell you were near the shore without looking?" I asked.

He pointed up the shore a bit. "I use that old stump as a land mark. When I pass it I slow down." I thought he must have to remember a lot of landmarks with all the lakes there were around here.

This time we got out of the boat, and my legs were so stiff I had to be helped. My father unloaded and handed me my gun and my case. He had carried them both before."Now you get your first lesson in using a gun." he said. "Don't let it get dirty and always carry it so that it doesn't point toward anybody. This is important. You need to learn how to behave with it before I give you any ammunition or teach you how to shoot."

I suddenly realized I could kill someone with this gun even without meaning to, or shoot myself if I wasn't careful. And there wouldn't be a doctor to come help. I was sure of that.

When he had the boat emptied and the oars and paddle stowed back under the seats he pulled out a thing I hadn't noticed before. It looked like a yoke farmers use on oxen. He tied it to the boat. Then he reached down and lifted the bow of the boat and turned it upside down over his head. The stern was resting on the ground and he backed his way toward it until he was amidships and just under the yoke. With the boat resting on the yoke and his hands holding the gunwales in front of him, my father set off down the path. He was carrying his pack-basket.

Everyone carried one of these except me. The Graysons had brought supplies with them: potatoes, flour, sugar, coffee, tea, salt and bacon. This had been distributed between my father, Charlie and the Graysons. They also carried blankets, extra clothes and fishing gear. Somehow they managed to get it all on their backs or in their hands.

I got myself moving and before the walk was over I was pretty well limbered up. There were no hills, and I felt I could have walked much farther though I did stop several times to change hands with my case and gun. I had a good chance to get acquainted with the look and feel of that gun. It was shorter than others I'd seen. "Winchester" was printed in the metal of the octagonally shaped barrel. The cleaning rod was stowed in a hole in the stock. I was glad it was short for as it was, it was heavy.

The path ended at a small beach of sand and rounded pebbles. A stream ran down from the lakes we'd just left. It slowed down here and widened out enough to accommodate our boats. They were lowered into the water, loaded up and we were off. This time the paddlers had plenty to do and I noticed Elizabeth had changed places with her mother and was doing the work. She had a pleased look. I wondered when I would get a chance to do it.

The river flowed quietly in wide, meandering curves between low banks of heavy shrubbery. Trees grew close to the bank at first then receded to the distance. Our boats went shushing through patches of lily pads. There was a faint, sweet smell from the white lilies. I could hear the ladies fussing over them just around the last bend. The sound of their voices seemed to hang in the air a bit before going quiet. I was warm and sleepy, and if I could have found a way to make myself comfortable I'd have taken a nap.

When the river opened up into a lake the mountain

was still behind us, smaller but still dominant and very blue. My father put his oars back in the water and said, "That was Marion River".

I looked behind me and saw that we were in a big lake so I assumed that it must be Raquette. The water around us was still calm but ahead it looked angry. My father was heading straight for it then I realized he was facing backward, maybe he didn't know it was that bad. "Dad," I said, "the water looks really rough ahead of us."

He turned to look. "Oh, it's just a bit choppy, nothing to worry about. The lake doesn't stay calm much this time of day." He turned back to his rowing.

Mr. Grayson said, "Anything new going on here?"

"Several," my father said. "One you will really be interested in: Dr. Thomas Durant is building on the lake."

"You mean the railroad Durant?"

"That's right. He's put up some simple cabins just the other side of Long Point. Charlie and Ed Bennett have a cabin on the end of the point and are lodging people there. Durant called his son William back from Europe and sent him up here to supervise the building. He built near the Bennetts."

"Sounds to me like it may be more than just a summer home then. A man like that may have a plan for making money."

"It does have that sound. This lake's been pretty quiet all this time, now it's like people suddenly discovered the place. Maybe Dr. Durant has plans to build his railroad on up here from North Creek then cash in on the sportsmen. If he can build a railroad across the Rocky Mountains there's no reason why he should hesitate to build one here, as long as it would pay that is. I'm not sure that it would."

"I don't know about that," Mr. Grayson said. "I know lots of men who would come here if they could avoid the rigors of travel. As for me, I like the roughness of it. It keeps everyone out except those of us who really want to be here. I suppose it would be a good thing for you guides though, lots of business."

"I don't know. I have all the business I need. I guide because I like it. I like it because the ones I work for usually really want to be here." He grinned and said, "I'm not so sure your wife really wants to be here, though."

Mr. Grayson laughed. "Don't you worry about my Jane. She's having the time of her life, I guarantee it."

By now the spray was hitting me in the back, but the two men seemed unconcerned. The boat wasn't tipping much more than it had on still water. I concentrated on watching Charlie and the ladies.

They passed us and we followed them. Going north, we passed between an island and a point of land then out into a wide expanse of lake. I could see what looked like a small hotel ahead. I didn't see the cabin across from it on the other side of the lake, but my father pointed it out with a short "that's our place" as we passed on by.

The waves became even worse, but my father just pulled harder at the oars. I decided both men were crazy. Charlie must be crazy, too, probably every human being who lived in these woods was crazy. They would have to have something wrong with them to want to stay in a place where you must get everywhere by boat.

My father asked, "You know how to swim boy?"

"No."

"Well, I'm going to have to teach you first thing, I guess."

The rest of the trip passed without conversation, and I was left to think about the prospect of a swim. It was the last thing I wanted to do. It was undignified and unhealthy and the water was cold. Perhaps he didn't mean it. He must have been joking. It seemed to be his way. But in case he wasn't I began a list in my head of reasons why I shouldn't swim. They were very good reasons, and I was sure that at least half of them were of the type that no responsible person would overrule. By the time we landed I was fairly confident that I would not have to go into the water.

We landed at a place they called Stillman Bay on the west side of the lake. There was a lean-to there big enough for all of us and a stone ring in front of it for a fire. We ate the lunch we'd brought along from the hotel. When we were finished Charlie declared that it was the last easy food we'd have for a while and would anyone care to go fishing.

"That's what I came for," Mr. Grayson said, and he got up and flourished his rod like a soldier going off to fight a duel. "Are you coming, Dearie?" he asked his wife.

She guessed she and Elizabeth would stay ashore this time and make camp and look around.

"Well, son, I think you and I should give it a try and see if we can bring back a bigger fish than those two old men."

I was very relieved, for I thought he was going to suggest a swim. I was also a bit scandalized that he would call Charlie and Mr. Grayson old men right in front of them. I supposed it was all right with Charlie because they were friends and about the same age, but Mr. Grayson really was an old man. If he was insulted he didn't show it but only laughed.

"All right Chadwick, we'll meet your challenge. We'll not only bring back the biggest fish but the most as well."

We climbed back into the boats and were off in two different directions. I would have liked to stay behind and walk some of the stiffness out of my legs, but I didn't dare press my luck. I reasoned that if I decided I wanted to stay on land he might decide I should have a try at swimming. Better off on the water than under it.

"Charlie's going south, so we'll go the other way.

No sense in competing for the same fish." My father rowed us to a small beach and we got out.

"Is this where we fish from?" I asked.

"No, this is where we get our bait. We fish from the boat." He began moving slowly down the shore, picking up medium sized rocks from under the water with his left hand. I couldn't see what he was looking for until he picked up a rock and out shot a little creature he called a crayfish. It wasn't a fish though but some kind of crustacean. He grabbed it with his right hand as it tried to get away. It waved its pincers back and forth opening and shutting them, trying to get hold of my father's fingers. He handed it to me and said, "You hold it while I look for another one."

"Can't you kill it first?"

He laughed. "Just hold it across its back like this and it won't get you. It's best to keep the bait alive, the fish prefer it that way."

So I took it gingerly, making sure my fingers were curled up away from those claws. He caught six altogether and threw them into the bottom of the boat, telling me it was my job to see that they didn't crawl out. Sammy jumped into the boat and skittered gingerly to the very point of the bow where he lay with his back to us and one eye rolled back to keep his eye on our catch. It seemed clear he'd had at least one bad experience with these creatures.

We pushed off again, and I kept busy knocking the crayfish back into the center of the boat if they started up the side or toward me. I used a stick I'd picked up on shore, and every so often one of them would grab hold and dangle as I waved it back and forth across the boat. Finally my father told me if I dropped one overboard he would make me dive for it. I stopped for a while, but it was too tempting a sport, and I was soon back at it but more carefully this time. I'd made up my mind I wasn't going in the water for any reason. I didn't want to give my father an excuse to bring it up.

He stopped rowing at a spot that looked like any other to me. "This is the best place to catch lake trout." he said. He shipped the oars and caught up a crayfish. "This is the way you attach the bait to the hook," he said and he pushed the hook between two sections of the shell along the back then he curved it back up so it poked back up through the shell. He threw it into the water and began letting out the line.

I could see that he expected me to bait my own hook, and I wasn't excited about the idea. During the quick baiting of his he'd been nabbed at least three times and one of them had drawn blood. It was just a small prick, and he paid no attention to it. But I knew it would take me much longer to do it and my hands were smaller and softer. I sat and watched the five crayfish scrabbling around. They looked all claws. Finally I went after the biggest one with my stick. I had a plan.

It grabbed the stick with one of its claws, and I pulled it over to where I sat and set it between my feet. Quickly, before it let go, I pinned its free claw beneath one foot. I loosed the stick and pinned the other side. With the creature immobile I could go at it with the hook, which I did, taking every bit as long as I had expected. I threw my bait out and let out the line as my father told me. Then I waited.

I had heard about fishing here and there, eavesdropping on my grandfather and his friends. It had sounded like a noble and exciting sport. But either the fish bite more quickly in England or they left out the waiting parts in the telling. Here waiting seemed to be all there was to fishing.

While we waited my father told me about Charlie. He started by pointing out Charlie's place; The Wigwams, to the north of us. I had no trouble finding it as it was the only building in sight.

"I found out about this lake from Charlie," he said,

"during the war. You have heard about our war over here haven't you? The one they called the Civil War or The War Between the States."

"Yes," I said, "the war my Uncle John fought in."

"That's the one."

"You fought in that war, too?" I was surprised. My grandmother had always mentioned Uncle John's bravery and self-sacrifice but led me to believe that my father had no part in it at all.

"No," he said, "John fought and Charlie fought but I didn't. Not men anyway. I fought death-- death, dirt and stupidity." I wanted to ask him what he meant, but he went on. "Your uncle John and I never saw each other during the war, but I met Charlie in the hospital, he had dysentery. When he was well enough to talk he told me all about these north woods. He was from Massachusetts, but he planned on moving here someday."

"What did you have?" I asked.

"What do you mean?"

"When you were in the hospital, during the war."

"Oh I didn't have anything. I don't catch much. That's what comes of washing your hands. So Charlie headed in this direction, but he got caught up for a while teaching school down south of here in civilization. As it turned out we got here ahead of him, your mother and I. There weren't many people here then, not living here anyway, just a few like Chauncey Hathorn and Alvah Dunning. There was a town starting at Indian Lake and a town at Long Lake. But here, nothing. Until a year or so ago everybody just went through. Quite a few people going through, though. A fellow named Murray wrote a book about it, made it seem so romantic and glorious that everyone who read it wanted to come here. Not everyone who comes here likes it though." He grinned. "But you'll find out about that for yourself by the end of the summer."

At the time I thought he meant that comment as a

foreboding of what my life was going to be like. I thought he was going to make things rough for me. I found out later what he meant. Not all the sportsmen and travelers were like the Graysons.

I only caught one fish all day, but when everyone had compared, it turned out to be the biggest. Charlie caught four, which was the most anyone got. My father cooked them in a frying pan with some bacon for grease as fish have no fat to speak of. He made cornbread in another pan using bacon for that too and he fried up some potatoes. Usually the guides did all the cooking but Mr. Grayson didn't want to be left out of the experience. When I looked back on it later I realized that the Graysons were wonderful company. They were with us a week. I was beginning to feel like they were family when they left. I knew I would never convince them that they should take me away, so I didn't try. They liked my father too much and they liked the lakes and the woods.But I was very happy to hear they would be coming back next year. If I wasn't out of there by then it would be something to look forward to.

We left them off at Merwin's and then Charlie took off to meet a client in Long Lake. My father had a week off before his next job. It was time, he said, to teach me a few things.

By now I was used to the guideboat. I should have been, for I was in it most of each day. It no longer felt tippy, and I'd learned how to move my weight and how to sit so it rode even in the water. I learned the hard way that when you move in a boat it moves in the opposite direction. I nearly ended up in the water once and my gun with me because I expected the boat to stay in place when I stepped out of it. I also knew why the guides didn't use rowboats. They would be too heavy and too ungainly to haul over the carries between lakes. They would also be too slow. The guideboats Charlie and my father had moved fast, faster than I would have thought possible with only one man rowing.

We went back through the lakes to Raquette and my father had me do the paddling from the stern. When we were on the Marion River he taught me how to use the paddle as a rudder and push with it at the same time. By the time we reached the lake I was pretty good at it. The lake was calm, so my father gave me a lesson in rowing. First we had to change seats. I sat on the floor between the seats while he stepped over me and sat down in my place, then I got up and sat facing him. It was no problem but a week before it would have terrified me.

Rowing was not easy because the oars overlapped in front. It was necessary to bring them back to me unevenly as I pulled, but my tendency was to bring them back together. I mashed my hands and bruised my knuckles before I had the proper motion figured out. I thought I was going along fairly well when I realized I was rowing in a circle. My right arm was dominating and was pulling us round to my left. Since I was not facing forward it took me a while to realize what was happening. My father wasn't paying any attention. He was reading David Copperfield.

"It's all right," he said when I complained that I couldn't see where I was going. "Just look back over your shoulder every now and then. I won't let you run into anything."

I plugged along this way until the sun began to go down. My father closed the book and said it was time to be getting on home. I gratefully gave up the oars and changed seats. My arms and shoulders were very tired from rowing and my legs from bracing myself.

For the rest of the trip I watched the sun go down in a blaze behind the clouds, turning them red. The trees became silhouettes, black against the sky. The taller ones, which I now knew to be pines, looked like they were all reaching across the water in the same direction.

It was quiet. For a boy like me, raised in the city, it sometimes seemed oppressively quiet, especially in the early morning or at sunset.

By the time we reached my father's cabin on Indian Point the sun was gone and there was only a rim of violet around the horizon. My father pulled the boat out of the water and turned it upside down. As we walked up the hill to the cabin I heard the sound of wood against wood and a voice came dimly across the water. I looked and saw some lights coming from Ike Kenwell's hotel. It was a relief to know there were other people somewhere near.

CHAPTER FIVE

The cabin was rectangular and was split into two rooms, a small one that was my father's bedroom and a large one which served as kitchen, sitting room and work room. The chimney was built in the wall where the two rooms came together, so there was a fireplace in both rooms. The back end of the big room was the kitchen and there was a little black stove with a pipe that went out through the wall. Up a steep ladder by the back wall was the loft. That was to be my bedroom, what part of it was not filled with wooden boxes. My father slept on a bed, but I had a mattress on the floor. A grown man would not have been able to stand in my loft at all. I could stand from the center where the peak of the roof was to about halfway to each wall. I didn't think much of my room until my father told me that some of the boxes held my mother's books. I was free to read whichever ones I liked.

But I didn't have much time for reading that week. My father kept me busy.

The morning after we arrived he took me outside to show me around. The privy I had seen of course. It was directly behind the house just within the trees. To the south of it, in the open, was a little low building. The floor of it was dirt and in one corner was a pile of evergreen branches with the needles still on. My father lifted the branches up to reveal a hole. I looked in and saw snow and the coldness of it hit me in the face. This was our ice box and I was given strict orders never to leave the hole uncovered or the door open. The shed also held tools and other odds and ends all hanging from the wall. He took down a hoe and left the shed with me then closed the door very carefully and latched it.

He took me to the south side of the house and I was surprised to see a large garden. I certainly had not pictured my father as a farmer and he apparently was not a very good one because all the plants were very small. The whole plot was edged by a row of little white balls which gave off a vaguely familiar smell. "What are those?" I asked, pointing to them.

"Mothballs", he said. "Helps to keep out the little animals. It doesn't work so well with the deer though. They are a problem. Sammy keeps them off fine while we're home but I have to take him with me when I go guiding."

"Why don't you build a fence?" I asked.

"Deer don't pay much attention to fences. They can jump higher than I can reach." He walked over to one end of the garden. It was covered with little mounds with sprouts of dark green leaves coming out of them. "This is the potato patch.Now, have you ever had anything to do with gardens?"

"No. I lived in London. It's a city. The farmers bring the food in from outside. But, isn't it very late to start a garden?"

"No. I planted about a month ago, as early as I could. We have long winters here."

He explained the rest of the garden to me and as it turned out half of the plants in the other parts of it were weeds and it was our morning's work to get most of them out. He showed me the vegetables, small and tender looking and growing in rows marked with a stick at each end. He went through with the hoe, loosening the soil between the rows and my job was to pull the weeds up by the roots and throw them in a pile. As the sun rose I became uncomfortably warm.

We hadn't half finished the weeding when my father stood up and said, "It's a good warm day. That should make for some good growth. I guess it's as good a time as any to take a swim. Time for your first lesson."

I contemplated running, but I was sure he could move faster than I, and I would eventually have to face up to him. There was no place to go and I was dependent on him for everything. So I simply said, "I don't want to."

"You don't want to go in the water on a warm day like this? You'll change your mind as soon as you get the hang of it. Soon you'll want to be in swimming every chance you get."

"The water is too cold," I said. "it's an unhealthy form of exercise. It could give me ague or consumption."

He burst into laughter and sounded for a while like he was going to choke. When he gained his composure he said, "Did your grandparents tell you that or did you just make it up on your own?"

I was indignant and embarrassed all at once, and I didn't say a thing.

"Come on, confess, you just made that up didn't you. Well, no one ever got the ague from swimming, much less consumption."

"People drown swimming," I said. My face felt hot.

"People drown more often because they can't swim," he said. "I know several men who guide on these lakes and don't know how to swim. That's asking for trouble. I'd be a poor father if I let you go even one summer without making sure you can at least keep yourself up in the water."

I wasn't convinced, and it must have showed because he said, "Come on down now and give it a try. I don't want to hear any more arguments." His tone of voice reminded me of my grandfather. I followed him to the shore and watched as he undressed down to his underclothes.

"Used to be able to go swimming naked before Kenwell put up his hotel over there. Now you never know who might be watching."

I didn't want anyone watching me in my underclothes and I was cooler now that we were by the water. "I'll just keep my clothes on."

"You need to learn how to swim without them before you can swim with them," he said. "Besides, there's nothing more uncomfortable than heavy wet clothes clinging to your body. Here, watch this." He plunged into the water head and all, did a somersault and came up lying on his back in the water. I stepped down onto the rocks and tried the temperature with my toe. It was cold.

"The best way is to get wet all at once," he yelled.

I sat down on a rock that was just under the surface. The water lapped at my stomach, and I held myself with my arms and shivered. My father dived and bobbed up feet first. He was obviously enjoying himself. I suddenly saw myself like I was someone else looking on. I looked silly. I'd been fighting the idea of living my father's way of life so hard that I was acting like a sissy. I felt ashamed. If I'd been on an outing with the boys at my school I would have been the first asking to row the boat. I would have baited the hook with my bare hands even if I did get pinched. Just thinking about this past week and all the things I hadn't wanted to do made me squirm. What had the men thought of me. I jumped to my feet and splashed into the water. I didn't realize the bottom of the lake dropped down so suddenly. I thrashed and kicked a moment as I felt nothing but water below me, then my foot hit a rock and I stepped onto it. I could stand with my chin just above the water. My father came up for air and I yelled, "I'm ready for a lesson now." I would do my best to carry out my plan to get back to London and continue my education, but I wanted to prove myself in the meanwhile.

By the end of that week I could keep myself up without having to touch bottom, and I was enjoying the water very much.

I was not so keen on weeding, but the shooting lessons I looked forward to. My father was very particular about safety and repeated many times that I must always treat the gun as though it were loaded even if I was sure it wasn't. I must never point it at anything unless I wished to shoot that thing. In spite of all his advice I came very close to shooting myself in the foot one day when I was practicing alone. The gun was not as long as most I'd seen, but it was heavy. I let it fall to my side and it discharged into the ground beside me. I had to sit on the ground and wait for myself to stop shaking. I was much more careful afterwards. It terrified me to know that we were probably days from a doctor. I never told my father about my near accident.

Things had become much easier for me, but I was often lonely. One afternoon between chores I was looking through my mother's boxes, trying to find something she might have put her mark upon when I found an old photograph. It was a family portrait, a man and a woman, two boys and a little girl. What I saw first was that one of the boys looked very much like me, but it was not me. The photo was too old and the boy was definitely older than me. I looked at him a long time before I noticed that the parents were my grandparents, younger than I had ever seen them. I was sure it was them. The lonely feeling grew stronger and I wished I could turn back time and have them with me again.

The picture made me uneasy, almost frightened. The boy that looked like me must be my father, but why was he with my grandparents who hated him. I remembered him telling me that his parents had died when he was twelve. I considered what might happen if I asked my father about it. He might get angry, he might simply tell me it was none of my concern. But that's what my grandmother would have said. My father was nothing like my grandmother.

I asked him that night as we ate if he'd known my mother's parents when he was a boy. I tried to be casual about it, but I was very nervous.

"Did you find the photograph then?" he asked.

"I found one that looks like my grandparents when

53

they were younger and three children. One of them looks like you."

"It is me."

"And the other two are my mother and my Uncle John?"

"That's right. I hadn't realized until I met you that your grandmother hated me so much she didn't tell you anything about me."

"She told me it was your fault my mother died."

He'd been looking at his plate, and his head shot up in surprise. "So that's how she saw it. She never said that to me. And your grandfather let her tell you that without saying anything. I'm surprised..." He sat quietly for a minute, thinking. "No I'm not surprised. She always did rule the roost." He looked at me intently. "I'll tell you what killed your mother. A doctor came to the house to deliver you. He came in a hurry from the bedside of a very sick person and never washed his hands. She caught an infection and within two weeks she had died. I wanted her to stay here to give birth and if she had she would be alive today."

I was stunned and sat silent for a long time trying to take this in and trying to decide which side I was going to believe, his or my Grandmother's. Finally my original question came to mind.

"So what were you doing with my grandparents when you were just a boy?"

"My father and your mother's father were business partners. They were very close, and our families spent a lot of time together. When my parents died your mother's parents took me in and raised me."

Nothing would have surprised me more than this. But the photograph was there, and I couldn't deny it must be true.

"Were you and Uncle John ever friends?"

"We've been friends all our lives."

"You mean he's still your friend?"

"Oh yes, but we've chosen very different ways to live, so we don't see each other often anymore. John turned out to be much more like your grandfather than I thought he would be."

I wondered what he meant by that, but I didn't think about it long. There were too many other things that were more important. My grandparents had raised my father, for at least part of his life, anyway. He must have been like a son to them. If a careless doctor had really been responsible for my mother's death then why did they turn against my father? If my father and uncle were good friends then my theory about my uncle sending me to the woods to get rid of me and get my money was probably not true. Why hadn't anyone told me any of these things before?

It made me feel better to know that my mother hadn't married some stranger. She must have known him nearly as well as anyone could.

When I'd recovered from the shock of all this I felt much more at ease talking about my mother and my Grandparents, and I asked my father about his childhood.

"I grew up in New York City," he said. "But my parents took me on trips to Europe and the Holy Land and to the country, camping and hunting. We went to Maine often. My father loved the coast there.Mother preferred Switzerland, but she was happy any time she could get out in the open and walk."

He talked willingly about my mother. She was five years younger than my father and Uncle John. Mostly he told me things about their childhood.

One day I opened a box that was filled with books on anatomy and medical procedures, all very detailed and boring. Some of them had Mary Van Dam Chadwick written inside the cover. I asked my father that day why my mother had owned all those medical books.

"She wanted to be a doctor."

"A doctor!" I wondered if he was joking with me. His face, however, was quite solemn, "But women can't be doctors." I said.

"Why not?"

I just stared at him for a minute. I was not thinking why not, I was thinking, "Is this man crazy?" I could see he was waiting for an answer. "They just can't, women don't do those kinds of things."

"Why don't they?" he insisted.

I was confused. "I think, I suppose it's against the rules."

"What rules?"

I didn't know the answer to this. I just said, "Well, in England it's not done."

"It's not done in America either," he said, "at least not often. But why? Are there really any rules that say they can't? Do you think women aren't as smart as men?"

"Of course they aren't as smart."

"Do you think then, that your grandmother wasn't as smart as your grandfather?"

That was a hard question. Of course I'd never thought of one or the other of my grandparents as being smarter. They were just different. "Well, my grandfather was smart about different things." I was getting angry. I felt sure I was right, and I was also sure my grandmother would have agreed with me, but I couldn't think of a way to back up what I believed.

"You need to think about this for a while," my father said. "But I think you should know this: Your mother was a very intelligent woman, and she would have been as good a doctor as any man if she had lived."

I went up to my loft and took out the photograph of my mother I'd carried with me from England. She was young and beautiful and dressed very well. She had been sought by many rich men. My grandmother had said so. How could a woman like that want to have a job that only a man should do?

I put the medical books away and decided I would just not think about it. It confused me too much.

But my father wasn't going to let me forget. The next day he brought the subject up saying, "It sounds to me that your grandmother did a very good job of teaching you to think like her. You know Will, one of the reasons your grandmother turned against me was because I encouraged your mother to challenge old ideas. I felt that if your mother wanted to become a doctor and was willing to do the work--double the work of a man because she would have to prove herself over and over again--then she should do it. Her mother called us both renegades and said I had put the ideas in Mary's head. Who knows, I may have. We were children together, and I don't remember all the conversations we had."

"The other reason your grandmother hated me in the end was money. She claimed I tricked her into thinking I was going to become a rich man and then, as soon as I had Mary as a wife I changed. I told her money wasn't everything. I quoted scripture to her. I said 'it is easier for a camel to go through the eye of a needle than for a rich man to enter the kingdom of God.' She slapped me and called me a hypocrite. I must say she was right about that for I'm not a religious man." He laughed and shook his head. After a moment he said, "Your poor grandmother, she did care so much about money and influence."

It was a new idea to me that anyone would not care about those things. I suspected it wasn't true. Probably my father had failed at whatever he had planned on doing. Maybe he hadn't passed his exams at school. Maybe that's why he encouraged my mother to become a doctor. She could earn the money. But who would go to a woman doctor even if she could do the work?

CHAPTER SIX

In spite of his strange ideas I liked my father more as the weeks went by. Most of our time was spent guiding. I became quite familiar with the lakes we frequented. We went north through Forked and Long Lake all the way to Saranac Lake, and east through Utowana, Eagle and Blue. Occasionally we went west through the lakes that were called the Fulton Chain. These were numbered from one to eight.

Some of the clients were as unused to living in the woods as I was when I first arrived. Most were demanding and expected my father to do everything for them. We didn't guide parties with women often. But when the women were there the men seemed to do more for themselves and ask less of my father.

The Graysons hadn't brought guns. They were interested in fishing and looking at the scenery. But most of the men my father guided wanted to hunt. They didn't even have to leave the boat. Sammy was the one who did the work, along with any of the other dogs that happened to be along. My father set Sammy loose on shore and off he'd run. When he scented a deer he'd start to yip, sometimes so far off we could barely hear him. He'd try to head the deer toward us.

We had to stay quiet and far enough from land so we didn't spook the deer. It nearly always took to the water to get away from the dog. When it had swum a ways out we'd get between it and land. The patron shot it from the boat, often with the gun right up against the deer's head. It was dragged to shore or on occasion hauled into the boat.

It was important to be close to the deer in summer because they sank fast, not having their buoyant winter coats. There were even times my father held the deer by the tail while the patron shot it. Even then sometimes the hunter would be so nervous he'd miss.

My father often left me at camp during these hunts, especially if he thought the patron was too inexperienced with a gun or too excitable. I hated being left behind. I could hear the dogs and the gunshots and I could sometimes see the boats, but never clearly enough to tell what was going on.

One day we were camping on Forked Lake with a party of six; three men and three women. There were three guides. My father and the other two guides took the men out for a hunt and the ladies and I stayed at camp.

Forked Lake is all bays and points so the boats were out of sight in a few minutes. A little later we heard the dogs. One even came our way for a time. We heard several gunshots.

When the men came back the deer was in my father's boat, dressed out. My father and the man he was guiding lifted it out and hung it by the antlers to a tree branch. This patron's name was Wilfred and he was in the habit of calling my father his "mighty servant". That annoyed me terribly, but my father seemed to think it was very funny.

It was obvious when they came ashore that Wilfred was pleased with himself. He was anxious to tell the ladies how he'd done it.

"Oh my dears", he said, "how I wish you could have seen it. The noble animal burst forth from the forest and stood poised on the rocky outcropping at the end of the peninsula. His chest and sides were heaving, but he hesitated only a moment before he leaped majestically into the foaming waves."

I wondered about that. Our part of the lake had been fairly calm all day.

"We waited for the animal to distance himself from the shore. Then at just the right moment my mighty servant leaned hard upon his oars. Our boat was nearly lifted from the water with the force of his rowing. The wake from our boat rose to the height of our shoulders. In a few strokes we were between the beast and the shore. It turned in confusion then turned again. Our boat was tossing and the animal shifted his position unceasingly yet I was able to take aim and with one shot put a quick end to the confusion and misery of the noble beast."

As a quick afterthought he added, "Our dear Charles and Mason were unfortunately too far from the spot where the deer came to water. They missed all the action."

"Oh well, better luck next time, right Mason?" Charles said. "Bravo Wilfred." The men and the ladies clapped and Wilfred took a little bow.

They were such pleasant people and Wilfred was so eloquent. I envied them their carefree, elegant life. But I hated knowing that they thought of me only as the son of the mighty servant. They never called me or my father or the other guides by name the whole time they were with us.

My father's job was to wait on people, take care of them and see that they had fun. He *was* a servant. I supposed it might be easy enough to bear if you were raised all your life the child of a servant. But I was from a wealthy family, brought up to expect an education and to be able to have a profession that would gain me respect. Being like a servant to these men humiliated me. I wanted them to know I was as good as they were. I had traveled in Europe. I had been raised in London. It was embarrassing that my father put up with their attitude with such lack of dignity.

The idea of becoming a doctor had been forming in my head since I learned my mother wanted to be one. I still didn't approve of a woman being a doctor, but I thought it was noble and grand of her to try. Instead of being a lawyer I could fulfill her dream for her. Now, humiliated from being treated like a servant, I thought of how much people depend on doctors. Their knowledge is something everyone looks up to. If I became one people would call me Doctor Chadwick, not their mighty servant. I formed then a firm resolve to go to medical school.

However, my new aspirations did not keep me from looking forward to my first hunt. My father said I was ready as far as my gun practice went. We only needed time alone. My first hunt would be at night.

The time came late in August. We were at the cabin for three days between jobs. On the second night, after we'd eaten our supper, my father said, "Tonight is the night you get your deer. Get your gun, we're going jacking." He took out his jacking light. I'd seen it before but not in use. It was a candle on a stick with a semicircular shield of birch bark around it.

I loaded my pockets with ammunition.

"Don't worry about that son," he said. "One shot is all you get on a night hunt. After that the deer is gone and all the rest within earshot. This animal won't be swimming.

Still, I took five rounds just in case.

We shut Sammy inside and made our way through the dark to the shore. "You'll have to paddle from the stern, can't use the oars for this," my father said. "Be as quiet as you can. Don't lift the paddle from the water and don't rub it against the boat. I'll sit in the bow with the light. It stuns them, fascinates them. They can't see us because the shield keeps the light from shining on us. When the deer freezes that gives you the chance to pick up your gun and get off a shot. Don't get too excited about it though. I don't want you to shoot me in the back."

We went north, sliding along close to shore with the light shining the whole way. I kept my eyes on the edge of the trees even though my father said we'd have our best luck when we were out of sight of Kenwell's hotel. We rounded the end of the point and started into Sucker Brook Bay.

I was more experienced with the paddle than the oars, still the effort to paddle quietly was putting a strain on me. I was reaching out away from the boat to keep from banging and my shoulders and thigh muscles ached. I was trying to shift ever so slightly to relieve the pressure on my legs when I saw an eye glowing. Was it a deer? It was too close to the water, maybe a fox or a beaver. The eye moved up abruptly, just a bright light hanging in the dark. It had to be a deer. It had been drinking then raised its head up to look at our light.

I stopped paddling and wanted to grab the gun on my lap. But what should I do with the paddle? I couldn't hold it and shoot and I didn't dare lay it in the boat. That always made a noise. Finally I lowered it until it was floating on the water then I let it go.

I raised the gun slowly and took aim at the neck. I was now able to see faintly, arching over a patch of water lilies. The noise of the gun was terrible in the soft, watery quiet. The deer reared, turned and leaped to the shore then dropped to the ground. Its legs thrashed a bit then it lay still.

"Good shot son. I thought you'd never get it off though, what kept you?"

"The paddle. I had to drop the paddle in the water. I'm afraid I've lost it."

My father laughed. "It can't be far away. That deer won't be going anywhere. We'll find the paddle first."

I let my father take over. I was suddenly cold and shaking. I had got my deer with one shot. I decided I liked night hunting. But I would be glad to get to bed.

My father dressed it out there while I held the light. He saved the heart and liver and left the rest of the insides for the little animals. We loaded the deer into the boat and carefully placed the feet. It was a doe so we didn't have the usual worry about the antlers piercing the thin siding.

When we got home my father hung the deer by the front feet from the roof inside the shed. We had the heart for breakfast fried. At supper we had chops and potatoes. The next day we had liver with onions and bacon and my father cooked up a roast to take with us since we had to be leaving in the morning. We sold the rest of the deer to Ike Kenwell for a dollar, and I got the money. I was glad to have it, but I hated to leave behind my first deer. I was all for wrapping a pile of the raw meat to take with us.

"We couldn't eat it before it went bad. It is a pity though. It was a good tasting deer. The does usually are. You'll get used to it. It's only the ones you shoot in winter you can keep till they're gone, unless you make jerky of it. That takes too long." So I pocketed my dollar and we left my deer behind.

For the next four days we guided a man named Jules. He was with his friend Sam. I don't know why they were together. They were about the same age, but that seemed to be the only thing they had in common. We met them at Holland's on Blue Mountain Lake, and Charlie was there too, guiding for Sam. When we arrived Jules was complaining about the stage ride. I helped my father carry his gear to the boat. He was carrying too many clothes for a four day trip. Jules told us where to put everything and how to carry it, fussing all the while about the water and the small size of the boat. But he didn't carry a thing. My father ignored him as best he could and stowed everything where and how he wished. He had to keep the boat level.

Sam was a pleasant man, almost jolly, and tried to engage my father and Charlie in conversation, asking things about the weather, trees, mountains, names of the lakes, etc. I say he tried because on every topic Jules would break in with a complaint and a comparison: The weather was too wet and chilly at night, Albany had a much better climate. The trees were too close together and the mountains much too low and wooded, not like Switzerland where the mountains were real mountains and the natives kept the forests decently trimmed. There were far too many lakes and streams. It made traveling difficult, not like the Lake country of England where things were better arranged for convenient travel.

I was indignant and wanted to say something. Not only was he complaining about everything but he was acting as though we didn't know anything. I wanted to say, "You're not the only one who's been to the Lake Country and Switzerland.

The next thing Jules found to complain about was me. When he discovered I was to be traveling with them he was very put out. "I am a world traveler," he said. "I have been to India and the interior of Africa. I didn't come here to be kept back by a boy." My father let Jules rant but when he stopped for a breath he broke in.

"I can see that you would probably be happier with someone else," he said."I think you can get yourself another guide if you wait a day or two at the Hotel." He reached into the boat and started lifting out one of Jules' bags.

Suddenly I felt like I was a trouble maker. My father would lose this job and it would be my fault. But it didn't happen. Jules spluttered a bit then climbed into the boat. Whatever world traveling he'd done, he hadn't been doing it in boats. He was worse than I was my first time, and even sloshed some water over the side onto his precious cargo.

My father put me and Sammy in the bow and Jules in the stern. That is the way we traveled the whole four days they were with us. It made things difficult for my father as he had to look at Jules the whole time and had to let him paddle on occasion. But it was much easier on me.

That first day out Jules complained continually

about the mosquitoes. He was terribly offended at the carry when my father asked him to help with the luggage.

"I charge 50 cents more every time I go back along the trail for extra gear."

"It's the first I've heard that." Jules said with a superior look on his face."I am not going to put up with expenses suddenly tacked on."

"That's fine, I don't mind taking you back."

It suddenly occurred to me that my father might be trying to get rid of Jules--money lost or not. If he was, it didn't work. Every time my father called his bluff Jules backed down. He carried his own things, or at least part of them, for the rest of the trip.

That night, while we were eating, my father said, "I knew a feller, moved here about seven years ago, city man, decided to be a hermit. First summer he stuck to the lakes and did all right. The second summer he decided he'd venture back in on foot a bit. He wandered into a swamp and the mosquitoes attacked him hard. He ran till he was free of the swamp then the black flies swarmed him. All in all he ran twenty miles to get to water deep enough to cover him then drowned from exhaustion." Jules believed it but I was pretty sure it was one hundred percent made up.

The next day we stayed on the water fishing. A climb up West Mountain for the view had been in the plan, but Jules preferred to fish.

That night, as we were fixing our cornbread, fish and potatoes, a mild thunderstorm rolled in and forced us under the lean-to roof.

"You know, it was just this kind of night about five years ago when I had a run in with a hail storm." My father looked up into the sky. "We don't get a lot of hail here in the north woods, but when it comes it's bad. I was in the middle of the lake when it hit. "I had to dive into the water and cover myself with the boat. That hail was the size of potatoes."

"I was fishing off my dock when that storm hit." Charlie said.

"I had to dive beneath the dock and hold my breath. I barely escaped death another time when ball lightning came down and bounced into my lean-to. I escaped but the lean-to burned."

"Oh sure, lightning is bad here," my father said. "I had it strike the end of my oar and knock me clear out of the boat. The weather can get troublesome this time of year."

It was only a mild storm, a little thunder but no lightning we could see. But Jules was gaining respect for this part of the world. He questioned my father for half an hour about how we would get back to the stage line if hail or lightning ruined the boat. My father finally told him he had a spare boat in a shed a couple miles down the lake. I knew this wasn't true, but he needed him to let up on the matter so we could get to sleep.

It was a trying four days but meeting Jules did something for me. Watching a grown man acting so silly and making life so hard for everyone else made me feel more mature. I knew I could fit in and be helpful and even carry on a sensible conversation. After that I was less self-conscious about talking with adults and more confident when I tried something new.

CHAPTER SEVEN

By September the weather was turning colder, especially at night, and there were no more bugs. I enjoyed it but more and more of my father's patrons preferred to spend the nights at the hotels. This meant I had a chance to meet some of the people who lived on the lakes year round. I noticed some boys about my age at Long Lake but never got close enough to meet any of them. I wondered if they had a school.

I liked to sit on the porches and listen to the men tell stories but more often than not my father sent me inside to do chores for the women. It was usually the wives who had to fix the meals and keep the places fit for the patrons to sleep in. I hauled water and washed dishes. When we were at Charlie's Hattie Blanchard sent me outside with her little boys to keep them out from under her feet. Sometimes I'd get a treat for my work, maybe a piece of cake or pie.

It seemed that everywhere we went people were talking about Dr. Durant and his son William. Even as far north as Saranac Lake the hotel owners asked my father about them almost as soon as he got his feet propped up on the porch railing.

"Well Ben, you think we're getting a railroad in here? Is Durant telling you anything?

"No sir. He keeps his own council. It's mostly his son that comes up anyway. He's doing plenty of building. Must miss Switzerland. That's what his place is going to look like, the kind of houses he's putting up. But we don't cross paths much."

The truth was, my father seemed to avoid running into anyone at that place. We went past there several times during the summer but we never stopped. There was always a lot of activity going on. Once he did point out William Durant. He was standing apart watching the work, tall and slim with dark hair and a mustache, very distinguished looking. I was sure my grandfather, if he had been living on the lake, would have made an effort to be social. We would probably be asked to look around the buildings and perhaps be invited to tea.

I supposed that because my father was simply a poor local guide he would not be welcome. My father probably knew this and that was why he merely passed on by. I felt I belonged with rich people and longed to have my own boat so I could go there myself.

But I didn't really have time for visiting. Between jobs we had work to do at home. First we brought in the squash. A light frost had withered the leaves and my father wanted them in before a hard frost hit. We scattered them around my bedroom, on the boxes and the floor. We dug most of the beets, turnips and carrots and buried them in the dirt floor of the shed. The rest we left in the ground to eat before the snow came. We started digging potatoes. These we spread out on the porch to dry, then we put them into cloth sacks and laid them in my father's room.

The next day off I thought we'd dig the rest of the potatoes but we went looking for wood instead. We went in the boat and hugged the shore like we were jacking deer, but it was broad daylight.

"We're looking for logs washed up, or dead trees," my father said. "It's a lot easier floating them home than hauling it in from the woods. It takes a pile of wood to keep the place warm all winter.

We found two logs the first day and floated the second one home behind the boat.

The log we took the next day had a symbol stamped into the end of it. My father tied it to the stern and gave it several feet of rope. "We don't want it bashing into us on the way," he said.

It slowed us down a lot and we took most of the morning getting it back. But rolling it up from the water onto our rocks was the hardest part. My father had a tool called a peavey that he hooked around the log to lift and roll it. He got one end up and it was my job to hold it there while he rolled the other end. I lost my grip on it twice and got a nasty bruise on my shin the second time.

"Guess we'll have to do it the old way," my father said, and he left me to keep the log from floating away while he went up to the shed. He came back with a stout pole. When he rolled the log up I jammed the pole between two rocks to hold it. Then he rolled the other end up. When we got it to the grass he said, "We'll leave it there to dry and cut it up later."

"I wish we had a beach like Mr. Kenwell," I said.

"That would make things easier, wouldn't it? Pretty short sighted of me to settle on such an inconvenient spot. All that flat land over there, we could have all the garden we'd ever want."

The nights became very cold and sometimes the days were blustery with the lake whipped up into white caps. The water and the air became too cold for swimming. The maple trees dropped their bright leaves then the dun colored leaves of the beech and birch trees blew away with the wind. I was grateful for the evergreens because of the green they left us.

When the logs we gathered had been out of the water a couple of weeks my father sawed them into chunks and we carried them up and stashed them in the shed.Some of the wood he split with a double sided ax. He showed me how to make the wood come apart on the grain by hitting the cut side of the chunk at a very slight angle then let me try it. At first I spent most of my time trying to get the ax out of the wood after I had driven it straight in. But I finally got the knack, I thought. I'd been working on pine. When my father gave me some beech to split the ax bounced off. He laughed but told me I'd better not try splitting any hard wood unless he was around.

I was beginning to know my trees. The ones with

needles and cones: pines, hemlocks, spruce and fir, were soft. They burned hot and fast and were easy to split or cut with a knife. We used that wood to get a fire started. The hardwoods were the maples, beech, birch, cherry and others that had leaves that fell off every year. These burned long and slowly, good for keeping a fire going all night.

Behind our cabin was a grove of beech and maple trees. My father took me back there and showed me how to find the little pyramid shaped beech nuts. He left me with a pail and went to split wood. It took me two days to fill the pail. We toasted the nuts on the stove a bit so they wouldn't mold. After that we both spent a day filling cloth sacks with dead leaves and carrying them to the garden. That was a mulch and improved the quality of the soil. That's what he said and though it didn't make a lot of sense to me I had to believe him. I certainly knew nothing about gardening.

When we had the wood all in it was time to go to Long Lake and bring home some supplies. "First we'll go on north of there a bit." My father said. "There's a new saloon keeper I've heard about. They say he's a good one to trade furs to."

It was a calm, clear day for our little trip and we made good time. We pulled our boat up on shore just a little north of Long Lake village and walked up a small dirt road.

When we went into the saloon it was quiet. Several travelers were having a meal at one end of the room. My father and the owner, whose name was Moose, got into a detailed conversation. I wasn't interested in pelts and prices, so I went off to sit by a window. I was watching a man cut hay in a nearby field when suddenly there was a commotion at the other end of the room. Someone yelled. One of the guides was swinging a large knife back and forth in front of another one. Their patrons had scattered, one out the door and the other to the back wall. The one guide was just standing back and keeping his distance as the other one called him names and waved his knife. I hadn't been around drinking men much, but I guessed the knife waver was drunk. He was also dark and had a strange accent.

Sammy pushed in behind my legs and whined. It was the first time he'd come to me for anything.

"OK Johnny, you'd better cool your heels because I've got my gun cocked." Moose nonchalantly laid his gun across the bar pointed more or less in the direction of the man with the knife. The rest of the men scurried out the door and Johnny left slowly, cursing and shaking his head.

Moose laughed, "Those Injuns, they're mean when they get a skinfull."

"Why do you give him the liquor?" My father asked.

"Oh hell, Johnny's a good customer. I just keep my gun loaded and never let him in here with his. We get along just fine." He grinned.

We left then. We were almost to the boat when my father said, "We don't need to be doing any business there."

I was glad of that. I didn't want to ever see that Indian again. I wasn't all that excited about Moose either.

It was a relief to be back on the water away from that place. And Kellogg's, where we picked up our supplies, seemed warm and friendly and familiar.

CHAPTER EIGHT

We spent most of our time at the cabin now. My father had just one guiding job in November and that lasted only three days. Often the wind blew so hard even my father preferred not to go out on the lake if he didn't have to.

My father dragged the big wash basin in from the shed for us to bathe in. He leaned it against the wall behind the stove and said it would stay inside until the lake warmed up again in the spring.

Most days we stayed in and mended our clothes and tools or made things from scratch. I took a special pleasure over these indoor jobs. Some things my father let me make alone. He made himself a pair of rabbit skin mittens with the fur on the inside. After I watched him, I cut and sewed my own.

My biggest project was my snowshoes. My father had a pair hanging in the shed. All summer I had supposed they were part of some strange American game, for to me they most resembled tennis racquets. Now I found they were strapped on the feet for walking on top of the snow. I didn't understand why we needed to walk on the snow. Walking through it had never seemed that much of a problem. But my father said they were necessary, and he already had a pair started for me. Wooden frames had been steamed and bent to form the shape. My father cut grooves in the wood to hold the rawhide lacing in place. I did the lacing, using my father's as a pattern. This took days because I had to take the first one apart many times before I got it right.

My father hauled in his traps and checked them over to be sure they were in working order.

We'd been getting some snow off and on for weeks. It was cold enough now that I hated using the privy and only went out there when I couldn't wait any longer. My father called me down to the shore one windy day.

There was a good swell on the lake, and I was hoping he didn't want me to go out in the boat with him. It was too cold.

He pointed at the water. "Does the lake look any different to you?"

I looked, but I wasn't sure what he wanted me to see. The water was gray and uninviting, but it had been like that for weeks. Then I realized that though the waves were big, they didn't crest. "No whitecaps?" I asked.

"Good. Does the water seem sluggish to you? Do the waves seem to be going past slower than usual?"

"Yes," I shouted, suddenly aware of it and alarmed. "What's happening?"

"Lake's about to freeze. If we have a night without wind. Here." He handed me his oars, picked up his boat and carried it to the house. He slid it under the porch, put the oars in it and nailed the opening shut.

The lake didn't freeze that night, but when we went hunting the next day there was ice on Beaver Brook, up in from the lake where the wind didn't make it through the trees. The next night was still, but I was cold in bed and went down in the dark to curl up by the stove.

In the morning my father nudged me awake with his toe. "Cold night, wasn't it? Hope the squash didn't freeze."

I wanted to say, "What about me, I could have frozen up there too." But I didn't. After all, I was there by the stove and I hadn't frozen.

"Take a look at the lake," he said, and he went out the back door.

The front window was covered with frost, and I had to do a good deal of breathing and scraping before I had a hole big enough for looking. The lake was flat as a floor and shining, almost too bright to look at with the rising sun reflecting off it.All of it was frozen.

My father came back in with a piece of meat and

started cutting it up for breakfast. "Pretty good freeze," he said. "Now if the snow and the wind hold off for a few more days we'll be in good shape." He started slicing some potatoes. "If you had your own boat we could start trapping two months earlier. You could run a trap line while I'm out guiding. Give you something to do."

It seemed to me I had had plenty to do, but I liked the idea of having my own boat.

"You'll start getting paid now." He said. "Well, I guess that's not really true. You will start working for pay now. You won't get it until we take in our first load of furs. But you'll get one fourth of what we make if you hold up your end of the job."

As it turned out, trapping was a terrible way to make money. It was cold, hard, lonesome work. Often I had to kill the animal with a stick before I could take it out of the trap. It would have been there bleeding and in pain for a day or two, and just getting near it without getting bitten was a trick. I hated it. I would never have dared tell my father I didn't want to do it. But I spent many hours in imaginary conversation, trying to figure out how I would get out of it next year.

The trap line went up Beaver Brook and crossed over to Shallow Lake where my father kept a shack on the east shore. From there it went down Sucker Brook back to Raquette Lake and the north side of Indian Point. He took me with him the whole circuit several times until he was sure I knew where I was going and what I was doing. After that we would each start up a separate brook, meet at the shack and spend the night then head down the brook the other had come up. This way my father could check to see if I was setting my traps right.

At first my two greatest fears were getting lost and getting my hands caught in a trap. But the way was mostly on the flat, icy streams. It was only the one half mile between Shallow Lake and Beaver Brook I had to worry about. And as my father pointed out, I would have to go uphill to get lost. That would be too much work not to notice. As for the traps--I used my feet on them as much as possible and caught my boot heel so often it was part of the job. I managed to keep my hands out of harm's way.

Staying dry became my greatest concern. Many of the traps were set along the shore just under water. More were set in the swamps that bordered the brooks. It would have been easy enough on the snowy river banks to slide into the hole I'd chopped in the ice for a trap or break through weak ice in the swamp. I didn't want to try walking wet maybe 2 1/2 miles to the nearest shelter in below zero temperatures.

I carried a pack basket my father had bought for me, and at first my snowshoes were strapped to it at all times. My father insisted and I considered it a great burden. Then one morning it started to snow when I was part way up Sucker Brook. It became so thick I couldn't find the traps, so I got under the branches of a big Hemlock to wait it out. It was a warm enough day, so I napped. When I woke the snow was just falling lightly, but I couldn't walk out of my hiding place. The snow came to my knees. I strapped on my snowshoes and tried them for the first time. I was glad my father wasn't there to see me fall on my face over and over again as I tried to maneuver around trees and down banks. The weight of my pack basket held me face down in the snow as I struggled to find something to push against so I could get back on my feet.

It was a slow trip and I was fortunate that I only had one trap to empty. I did have to lay more bait at all of them because the snow had covered the old. I cut fresh branches for the beaver and laid down rotted meat or fish guts for the mink, muskrat and foxes.

It was nearly dark when I saw my father coming slowly toward me through the woods. He was sinking deep with every step in spite of his snowshoes.

"I see you weathered the storm," he said as he took my packbasket from me.

"I got under a tree and slept through it. Where's Sammy?"

This soft snow is too hard on him. I left him at the camp. It was a good idea to wait it out, you could have gotten lost if you'd tried to keep going. How'd you like your first day on snowshoes?"

I looked down and saw that my coat front was caked with snow. "I learned how to get up without taking them off first."

He laughed. "You got broken in the hard way. We ought to make it back to camp in good time. I've packed us a trail."

The cabin was warm and the smell of cooking meat filled the room. I ate until I nearly burst then fell asleep on the floor by the fire.

CHAPTER NINE

I made $90.00 that winter from the trapping. But by the time my father gave it to me I had nearly forgotten why I wanted it, so much happened that winter to involve me in my new life.

The weather became very cold, colder than I could have imagined. The snow squeaked under our feet and the vapor from my breath froze on the hairs inside my nose. I had to wear a scarf wrapped around my head so only my eyes showed. Distant booming sounds came from the lake. My father said it was the sound of the lake freezing.

We walked out on it one day and I heard a crackling, splitting sort of sound out beyond us. It became louder as it moved quickly toward us then it shot beneath my feet and went on in the distance behind us. I was terrified. I was sure the ice was going to crack beneath me and I would fall into the water.

Nothing happened. My father laughed. "Awful sound isn't it?"

"It sounded like the ice was cracking."

"It was."

"Why didn't we break through?"

"The ice cracks because it's expanding. That's the sound of ice being made. It can't open up, there's no place for it to go except up. If enough pressure is put on one spot a ridge will form across the lake. In the spring when the ice starts to break up those cracks will be the first places to open. Right now though, they are as safe as solid ground. But it is an awful sound."

The lake wasn't the only thing that froze in that weather. The meat that hung in the back shed was so hard my father had to hack pieces off with the axe. Some of our potatoes froze and two of the squashes. My father brought in our hides and covered the vegetables with them. It made my father's and my bedrooms smell pretty strong, but by then I was mostly sleeping on the floor by the stove anyway.

Twice I nearly froze my hands. My clothes were good and warm and my feet rarely got cold. I wore thick wool socks inside leather boots lined with fur. My mittens were warm too but just hide and fur. Twice I got them wet resetting traps and by the time I got to camp they were numb. The first time it happened I was unconcerned. But when I went to warm them by the fire I got the chill blains. The pain is awful. It feels like little needles are traveling through all the veins.

The second time I got my hands wet I tried very hard to keep them warm. But I fell twice and had to take them out of my pockets to get back up. After that my father made me a second pair of mittens and I kept them with me all the time.

After each round of the traps we spent two days at home. My father skinned the animals we brought back and stretched the hides. Sometimes I helped him. But often, if the wind wasn't blowing, I went ice fishing. I chopped a hole in the ice with the axe and sat reading while I waited for a bite.

One afternoon in late January I had a particularly good catch and it was all I could do to carry the fish and the book back up the hill to the house. I left the axe behind. My father had stressed that I must always put the tools back in the shed and lock the door. So far I had. But this time I just didn't see the need to go back for the axe until morning. I knew there wasn't a soul within miles. Why would anyone come prowling around here just in case I'd left something out. I left the axe and forgot it until about noon the next day when my father wanted to split some wood for the stove.

He was grim when he told me to go get it, but I refused to take it seriously. I was sure it would be there. My father was the strangest man, unconcerned about important things and wrought up over nothing. I supposed he was mad at me for disobeying.

The axe was where I had left it. The handle was chewed to a ragged mess, nearly through in places. It was certainly unusable.

"But why would anything want to chew on an axe handle?" I said to my father when I handed it to him. "There's wood all around us."

"The porcupines go for the salt. They chew on anything that is handled a lot by humans. Didn't you think I had a reason for telling you to lock everything in the shed?"

I didn't answer. The point to me was not that he had a reason, but why couldn't he have told me the reason in the first place. I would have been more careful.

"We can't keep warm for long without an axe," he said. "Tomorrow morning--first thing--you walk to Long Lake and buy a new handle."

There was not anyone I could think of between us and Long Lake. About fifteen miles of nothing but snow, ice and trees. Charlie Blanchard moved his family to Blue Mountain Lake for the winter. I went to bed that night hoping, praying that his anger would wear off by morning.

Angry or not, he was ready for me with a lunch and two pelts rolled up in my pack basket. "Get the axe handle and with whatever is left over get coffee, bacon and butter. Remember to pack the butter away from your body. Don't use the carry into Forked Lake. Just follow the river. Try to get back tonight, but if you think you can't, spend the night at the store. He has to keep the place warm all night so his canned good don't freeze."

I strapped on my snowshoes and left, still trying to think of a way out of my task.

I had been to Long Lake many times that summer in the boat, just along for the ride, not always paying attention to the landmarks. But all I had to do was follow the water, nothing tricky.

It's surprising how different things look in the winter. The woods are more open, the vegetation between the trees is covered, so the paths are not obvious. It was a good thing I didn't have to take the carry path. I never did spot it.

It was a strange thing to pass Charlie's place all empty and covered with snow. It was lonelier than the empty woods. Someone had been through with a horse and sleigh. I was following the tracks now. Probably Chauncey. He was the only one I knew with a sleigh on Raquette, unless it was Durant, up for a winter vacation. It made things a little less lonesome knowing someone had been through.

It was a windy day and I was glad when the lake narrowed down into the river and I was traveling closed in by the trees.

I was plenty mad at my father. It was about twelve miles to Long Lake, but another mile or two to the store. There wasn't a chance of me going both ways in one day and getting home in the daylight. I figured he had set me up-- never told me about the porcupines, so if I disobeyed him, something like this would happen. I guessed he must have been waiting, so he'd have a chance to teach me a lesson. I hated him right then almost as much as I had before I met him.

I reached Long Lake in the late afternoon. Mr. Kellogg, the shopkeeper, was fine about letting me stay the night. I had food with me, but not much was left by the time I ate my supper, so he gave me breakfast. There was money left from the furs and I offered to pay him.

"Naw, I'll take it out of your father's hide next time I see him." He sent me off with my purchases. Outside it was just getting light.

I was frustrated. I was in town and I hadn't seen anybody but Cyrus Kellogg. There was a school in Long Lake and I wished I could stay a day and go to it. I wanted to see if there was anyone my age around. I wanted to see what I would be learning if I could go to school. But tomorrow I had to run the trap line and my father needed his axe handle. Besides all that, I had no idea how my father would react if I got home a day late.

About two miles out of Long Lake I remembered the butter. I took my packbasket off and sure enough I had packed it on the side against my back. It was only slightly soft. I repacked it and went on. My load was a whole lot heavier than it had been the day before. Besides being more tiring, it also made me sink farther into the snow and that slowed me down. I was sitting on a log taking a quick rest when Chauncey Hathorn drove up in his sleigh on his way back to Raquette.

"Here boy, hop on up and I'll give you a lift home," he said as he pulled the horse to a stop next to me.

I gave it some quick thought. I was pretty tired, and I had about six miles to go. But I was sure my father had sent me on this trip as a punishment. If I skipped part of it maybe he would think up something else for me to do. So I told Chauncey thanks, but I'd better walk the rest of the way. He gave me a funny look, but he didn't argue.

I was so tired when I got back that I could scarcely make it up the hill from the lake. My father met me halfway and took my packbasket off me.

"I saw Chauncey go by here hours ago," he said. "Didn't he stop and offer you a ride?"

When I told him my reason for not riding he shook his head in disbelief then gave me a lecture on being too proud to accept help. It turned out that he knew when he sent me that Chauncey would be along to give me a ride. Seems he went up once a week to get his mail and usually came back the next day.

So maybe what happened two weeks later shouldn't have shaken me up as much as it did.

I set out on our trap line in the morning, crossing over to the north side of the point to go up Sucker Brook.

My father, who was faster than I, had a few chores he wanted to finish. It was a clear day with no new snow and only two traps to empty, so I reached the camp fairly early. I skinned the muskrat and mink I had caught. I was still new at the skinning, and I went slowly so as not to ruin the hides. It took me till past dark, and my father still hadn't showed up. I fixed my meal and went to bed. I slept uneasily and woke up twice to put wood on the fire and check for my father. He never came.

I was near panic when I set out the next morning. At each bend I expected to find him frozen to death in the path. But there was no sign he had even come this way. Two of the traps were sprung, one full, some needed to be baited. No new tracks came from the lake, though as I said, there was no new snow and I couldn't yet tell an old track from a new one.

When I got back to the cabin both my father and Sammy were gone. I only found one clue to what might have happened to them. Sleigh tracks passed close to the shore near the house. The snow there was so muddled with tracks I couldn't tell if he had gotten out or if my father had gone out to meet him. I was looking for blood, thinking he might have hurt himself, but I didn't find any.

He didn't show up that night or the next day and I was beginning to make serious plans about packing up some things and going to Long Lake for help. I didn't want to stay there alone indefinitely and someone else might have seen him or have an idea where to look for him. The second day I was cooking dinner when he and Sammy walked in the door.

I could tell right away something wasn't right. Sammy came right to me and leaned against my legs. He was clearly upset about something. It took me a few seconds to realize my father was drunk. "Where were you"? I shouted. "I thought you were dead or hurt somewhere."

"Now, what's the matter with you. Chauncey came by. He was on the way to pick up a shipment, and he wanted my help."

He was slurring his words. He came over to where I was cooking and served himself up a good plateful of venison, bacon and cornbread.

"No vegetables. Boy, you'll get scurvy if you don't eat more vegetables."

He ate a huge amount and talked the whole time, mostly gossip about people whose names I had heard but hadn't met. It was too rambly for me to keep track of or remember, but now and then he threw my mother's name in and said what a wonderful girl she was and how she'd have made a fine doctor if they'd have given her a chance.

If she had lived, I thought. But I never said anything. He just talked and talked until he fell asleep in his chair. I stoked up the fire and went to bed.

The next morning he was fixing breakfast as though nothing had happened. It was clear he was planning to walk the trap line. I showed him the three pelts I had stretched. He said I didn't do too badly for the first time.

This happened twice more that winter. I never saw him leave. He was always ravenously hungry when he got back and ready for work as usual the next day. He told me a couple of times that first year that Chauncey Hathorn was a terrible alcoholic. But he never mentioned drinking himself, and I never saw him with any liquor.

One day Chauncey came over in his sleigh. My father went down to greet him at the lake because our rocky shore line prevented him from coming to the house. My stomach went sour thinking about my father leaving. I hated those days being alone and uncertain, waiting for my father to come home. My father clumped in saying I should pack him some food. He went into his bedroom and came out again with something rolled into a flour sack.

"Charlie needs my help in Blue; Chauncey's going to give me a lift there" he said. "I don't know how long I'll be gone. If the weather gets bad stay close to the house and we'll check the traps when I get back."

That seemed different. He'd never expressed concern about my welfare or made any reference to how long he would be gone. Maybe Charlie did need his help. Chauncey lived near the mouth of the Marion River and that was closer to Blue than we were.

He came back in four days, sober. He said Hattie had another baby, a boy, and they named him John. That was all he said about it. He didn't say how old the baby was or what he had been doing at Charlie's.

CHAPTER TEN

The weather was getting warmer. Snow was melting and the brooks were showing through the ice in places. To my great relief we did our last round of the trap line, together this time. We gathered the traps and brought them home, cleaned them and oiled them and hung them inside the shed. The next day my father hauled out an odd assortment of cans and set me to work washing them. There were forty two altogether and each one had a hole just below the rim.

The trees around our cabin were plentiful and there were more kinds than I could identify. After picking all those nuts I would never mistake a beech tree for anything else. The white birch were obvious and I could finally tell the difference between the pines, hemlocks, cedars and balsam. I was about to get a lesson on the sugar maple.

When I had washed and stacked the cans my father grabbed a drill, a hammer and a bag of metal spouts and we dragged it all to the nearest maple tree. On the south side of the tree there were two holes, one almost grown in. On the same side my father made another hole with his drill at stomach level. He hauled a spout out of the bag. It was a tube with a hook on one side. He pounded the tube into the tree with the hook down. I slipped the hole of one of the cans over that hook on the spout. As soon as the can was hung, water started trickling out the spout and made a loud pinging sound as it hit the metal. Back and forth we went behind the cabin, hanging cans on all the maple trees we found bigger than about a foot in diameter. We always hung them on the south side of the tree because that side got the most sun.

When this was done my father built two short rock walls on a flat spot next to the cabin. He worked on those walls a long time getting them even. He set our wash tub on them over and over again to check. When the tub sat level between the tops of the walls he was satisfied.

"We'll have to take sponge baths for a while, this is the biggest pan we've got," he said with a grin.

He laid a fire under the wash tub but didn't start it.

"We're all set," he said. "Tomorrow we'll start making maple syrup."

It was my job to carry in the full cans from the tree and empty them into the wash tub over the fire. When there was about an inch of sap on the bottom of the tub my father lit the fire. After an hour or so it was bubbling every time I came to empty a bucket of sap into it. It smelled sweet.

If it started to snow we carried the tub up onto the porch. Usually we'd have to dip some of the sap out first so it wouldn't slosh over. Those times every pot we had sat around the house full of thin syrup. I wanted to boil it on our stove, but my father said it would make the inside of the house wet and sticky.

After several days I stopped filling the tub and my father let it boil down to where the taste satisfied him. We skimmed the scum off the top and filled wine bottles with the syrup. Then we started over again.

We had some warm days and the snow in the woods melted so that in spots the dead leaves were showing through. I went without snowshoes and I had to reach up to take the cans off the trees. The ice was getting rotten around the shore.

I was pouring my last can of sap of the day into the tub when I saw an unfamiliar man coming up the lake from the south. It was dusk when he got to our cabin and we were just beginning to cook our supper. My father said, "Hello, Frenchie, you're just in time to eat."

Frenchie was one of those types that don't mix conversation with food. When he'd pushed his plate away and leaned back in his chair, my father said, "OK, Frenchie, what is it? I know you're not here for a social visit. Not this time of year."

"You said it," Frenchie grinned. "The streams are getting pretty rotten. I had to cut across the swamp coming down the Marion."

"I usually hunker down here in the cabin from the first of April until the ice goes out," my father said. The next time I go up the Marion I'll be in my boat."

Frenchie shook his head and rolled his eyes. "Ordway sent me to get you. He's hoping you'll come back with me tomorrow. Says he'll pay you $30.00 if you'll stay with us till we get to North River."

"What does Jones Ordway want with me? I'm no riverman. I'm too old for that stuff."

Frenchie shrugged his shoulders and grinned, but he looked nervous to me. "He had a dream, a real bad one must be. Dreamed he'd lose 2 or 3 men on this drive. He just wants you around."

I couldn't figure out what they were talking about, but it made me proud to think just having my father around made people feel better.

"Jones doesn't need me yet," my father said, the banking ground is still frozen."

"But you have to get through before the ice starts to shift."

"We've got a few days. You can go back tomorrow morning. We've got some things to tie up here, got to finish our sugaring. You can tell Ordway I'll be bringing my boy along."

The next morning Frenchie set out after breakfast. I gathered up the pails and pried the spouts out of the trees. My father stayed close to the house, testing the syrup and washing out the pails I brought him. This time he boiled the stuff down very thick, much too thick for syrup. He said he'd make it into sugar when we got back.

"Where are we going?" I asked. "I didn't understand a thing you and Frenchie were talking about."

"We're going to watch a log drive. A whole winter's cut of logs is piled on the ice at Thirtyfour Flow. When the ice melts they open the dam and let the logs out. Drivers float them down river to the Hudson. It's exciting, a good thing for you to see, just as long as you don't decide you want to be a riverman. It's a hard way to make a living, gives most men rheumatism."

I was about to ask him why we had to go, but he pointed out over the lake. "See the far shore? See the black sort of haze just above the shoreline? That means the ice is melting, getting ready to go out."

It was a warm day. I'd been busy with the sugaring, so I hadn't been down to the lake in days. "Will it be too thin for us to walk on?" I asked. I didn't want to go anywhere on it. Frenchie had seemed too concerned about it.

"Thin," my father said, "oh it's not thin, it's just rotten, honey combed, full of little holes. It'll be a good 2 feet thick when it goes out. Dangerous time to be on the lake. But it's not time for that yet. We'll be all right."

I was puzzled. I'd figured the ice would just melt until it was gone.

The next morning we packed, put out the fire in the stove and left. My father said it could be a month before we got back.

There were bare spots on the hill in front of the house and the path to the lake was muddy. Open water lay between the shore and the ice. My father pushed a log out for the three of us to walk across on. Sammy skittered across fast, one of his back feet slipping into the water as he jumped to the ice. "Fall in that water and you'd better get out quick. Doesn't matter how well you can swim," my father said. He picked up the log and threw it back to shore where it clattered and bounced and lodged between two rocks.

The ice was wet and grainy. Several times we saw black holes. Two of them were big enough for a man to fall through.

"The melting ice makes pools of water that swirl around in the low spots and wear holes." My father said."That big hole is right over a rock that lies just below the surface. The dark rock attracts the sunlight and melts the ice."

We went ashore at Chauncey's. He wasn't around, but he'd left a plank between the shore and the ice.

"We'd better take our time getting there," My father said. "We'll have no peace once we get among the loggers and all the hubbub."

So we took a long route to the lumber camp, staying away from water and taking our time. We stayed in a trapper's cabin my father knew about. It was only maybe ten miles from Chauncey's to the Thirtyfour Flow, but it took us three days to get there.

When we walked into the camp fifteen men were there, all sitting around waiting for the ice to melt. I was told to go make myself useful to the two women who did the cooking. They had a fellow about 15 years old helping them, but they still found plenty for me to do.

Those two ladies were surely buzzing about my father being there. It was almost like there was some kind of secret about him. They kept saying how much better they felt, having him there, but they never said why. They were buzzing about Mr. Ordway too. Seems he was so rich he had 2 big houses, one in Glens Falls and one in North River. He was the big boss and didn't usually show up on the river, but he came this time to check things out and make sure everything went all right.

That evening my father took me to the dam. It seemed impossible to me that they would ever get all those logs through that narrow place.

It was good I had something to do while we were waiting for the ice to melt. Those cooks kept me pretty busy carrying water and wood and washing things. The men were going crazy. They played pranks on each other and dragged out each meal to break the monotony.

One of the lumberjacks, a young fellow named Jock, liked to pick on the cooks and complain about the food. He called me Limey and liked to try to mimic my accent.

"Young man," the head cook said, "if you're as tired of salt pork as you say you are and don't have anything to do but get in the way of the only busy people in the place, why don't you go out and get us some venison."

"Aw, come on," Jock said mournfully. "You know we don't have no guns here with us on the drive. I'd love to go hunting."

"Well then, the least you can do is go fetch us some firewood."

But we liked Jock. The cook said she thought he was lonesome for his mother.

When they were about ready to open the dam my father came to get me. "I'm going along the river with the rest of the men and from now on I want you to stay with me," he said.

They started letting water out a good half hour before they let the logs go. That was to get the water level up in the river--deep enough to carry the wood. A boom made of logs hung together with chains kept anything from going out of the lake early. When they released the boom some of the men headed down river with the first logs, others stood by the dam with pike poles and guided the upcoming logs through. We watched at the top for a while then followed the others.

One man rode the river balanced on a log. He used his pike pole to loosen any logs that got caught up on the bank. Another man rode what my father called a cooter; two logs tied together with rope. It was slower but easier to stay on. I was fascinated by the log rider. My father turned to me, "That water is ice cold," he said. "These men will all be crippled up by the time they're my age. It's a hard life."

Yet when Jimmy the cooter man left his stuff by the river to go talk to the boss, my father grabbed his cooter and went out among the logs, pushing stalled ones back into the current. Sammy whined and ran back and forth along the river bank. I thought my father was doing a good job, but behind me Mr. Ordway hollered, "Ben! Ben Chadwick you get off that river!"

He found a place downstream to get off and Jimmy was there in a minute to take over his cooter and pike pole.

I hurried to catch up with my father, but Mr. Ordway was ahead of me. When I reached him my father had a sheepish look on his face. He was saying, "All right, all right, I'm just not used to hanging around for days at a time without doing anything. It wears on me."

Mr. Ordway walked back to ride with the chuck wagon. My father and I continued down the river, keeping pace with the logs and the men on the river. I didn't ask him any questions. I figured he'd been humiliated. Nobody likes to be scolded. But I wondered why we were there if he wasn't supposed to help out.

The path cut off a bend in the river and left it out of our sight for a time. Where we met the river again there were several large rocks jutting out of the very middle. Jock was on them pushing the logs clear as they caught on the rocks. The water was moving pretty fast right there. As we watched, several logs came around the bend together. One stuck small end first between two of the rocks. The large end swung toward the shore and caught two others. It happened too fast for one man to keep up and in less than a minute there was a jam formed all the way to the bend in the river.

Jimmy and the log rider came along and tried to keep the jam from getting any bigger. They pushed off the logs at the upper end before they had a chance to catch. It looked like they might be gaining on it. Suddenly the log that started it all cracked under the pressure of all the logs and water. Its broken end kicked up and knocked Jock into the water among all the logs that had just been freed.

My father looked up and down the shore. I knew he was looking for something he could ride on, but there weren't any logs right there. He started to run downstream, and I tried to keep up with him and at the same time not lose sight of Jock, bobbing between the logs.

Jimmy had reached the mess now and was poling his way toward Jock. He grabbed him by the hair and one arm and pulled him over the end of his cooter. He made his way slowly to us, struggling against the current as he pushed his pole into the river bottom. I wondered if Jock was dead.

Out of the corner of my eye I saw the cook's wagon coming. I turned and saw Mr. Ordway running toward us. My father and Jimmy were hauling Jock onto the river bank. I could see there was a bone sticking out of his leg.

My father turned to us, and I didn't recognize the look on his face. I didn't recognize his voice either as he started giving orders. "Will, get me my pack basket, Ordway, I need hot water as soon as possible. Have someone build a fire. Get me blankets and clean towels if there are any. Clear off the back of that wagon."

He had always acted young and sort of carefree. With the clients in the summer he had seemed reluctant to ever be bossy. He was everybody's pal. Suddenly my father appeared older and completely in charge, like a soldier.

They carried Sam to the wagon and laid him on it, the broken leg to the outside. I stood ready with the pack basket. Jock sputtered and some water came out of his nose. He coughed violently for a bit then began a ragged breathing. "Well, that's that," my father said, "the first thing is to see to this leg. I'll need some help." He looked around a moment looking at people's hands then said abruptly, "Okay, Will, you've got small, nimble fingers, go wash your hands." He handed me soap from his packbasket, then followed me to the river and we both washed. "You've been reading your mother's books. Today you'll get some practical experience. You'll get to see the inside of a leg close up anyway."

I was awed and scared of him. He seemed so different, not the father I had gotten used to over the past year. But I still didn't catch on. I was wondering what my father could possibly do for this man. I was also hoping I wouldn't get sick.

Minutes later we were standing by Jock again. Someone had covered him with blankets and at my father's order towels had been put under his leg.My father opened up the cloth bundle I had seen once before when he had gone off to help Charlie. It was full of instruments: tweezers, knives, needles and thread. These had to be boiled. When they came out of the hot water my father started putting Sam's leg back together.As I watched him work I realized he had done it before, that this was what he did best.

I didn't get sick. I held skin out of the way, I mopped up blood and I handed him the tools. I tried to obey orders as best I could, but I was absorbed in watching. The books I'd been reading, the drawings and diagrams I studied, suddenly took on new meaning. This was what muscle and bone really looked like.

My father eased the two lower leg bones together as I held the torn skin out of the way. Then he stitched. The stitching took a long time. When he was finished he asked Mr. Ordway to cut him some saplings to make a splint.

My father felt Jock all over from his head on down to see if there were more breaks, but he didn't find any. He splinted the leg and wound it with cloth.

"What will happen?" I asked as my father washed his tools and wound them back up in the flour sack.

"He might get gangrene and then I'll have to cut the leg off. That's what often happens with that kind of break. But he was in the water and that water was clean and cold, maybe he'll be all right."

"Will his bones heal together after all that?"

"If we can keep him from moving it too much. He'll always be lame but he'll walk on it."

"How soon will you know if you have to cut it off?"

"Just a few days." He finished up and put his bundle back in his pack. "You saw that I put my instruments in boiling water before I used them and after."

"Of course."

"That's important, very important."

"Like washing hands?"

"Right."

"Why didn't you tell me you were a doctor. I feel really stupid, being your son, living with you all year, and I guess I'm the only one in the world who didn't know."

"People make too much of it. Doctors can't do much really."

CHAPTER ELEVEN

Jock kept his leg, but he had to give up log driving. "Best thing that could have happened to him," my father said.

We followed the drive to the Hudson where all the loggers met to take their logs on down to Glens Falls together. This was close to where I had started my stage trip last spring. The cook packed us up a couple of days worth of food and we started back home on foot. My father was a little richer but I was smarter and I looked at my father differently.

I had a question but we were almost back at Thirtyfour Flow before I had the nerve to ask it. "If you're a doctor, why did the one with the dirty hands do it? Why didn't you? I mean when I was born."

"I was out of the house. Your grandparents knew where I was but they didn't send for me."

"And you were close by?"

"Oh sure, no more than a mile away."

I wondered if he was out drinking but I didn't ask. He had never acknowledged his drinking. I had never mentioned it.

Thirtyfour flow looked lonesome with the buildings empty and all the logs gone. The dam was closed and the water sat flat and cold between muddy banks. We walked past it in silence. But there was something else I wanted to ask him.

"If you're a doctor, why do you let your clients treat you like some ignorant servant when you probably know more than any of them?"

My father grinned. "What do you want me to say? I'm a doctor so you'd better treat me with respect."

"Yes."

"Well, there are several things wrong with that. Usually, the more you know the less you feel the need to tell people about it. I don't really want people to know

I'm a doctor, and I hope you don't go around blabbing it to impress people. Doctors don't know much really. People think we can work miracles, then when we can't they get angry."

But I saw what he did for Jock's leg. That seemed like a miracle to me.

"Another thing is that doctors are servants. Anybody who doesn't like that idea should never become a doctor." He grinned again. "Besides, where did you ever get the idea that servants are ignorant? History is full of cases where the servant is smarter than the master. Lots of that even in the Bible."

I didn't answer him. I figured he was joking with me. Whoever heard of a doctor being a servant. It rankled me even more knowing that when people treated us like we didn't even have names, I wouldn't be able to say anything to them.

"We may not be able to get home," my father said. "Might have to spend a night or two at Chauncey's."

But when we got there the water was open and blue and it looked wonderful. Chauncey had his boats out of storage checking them for leaks. He offered to take us home right then.

While we were on the lake my father tried to get him to agree to make me some new trousers. Chauncey wouldn't do it. He said he'd had enough of sewing.My father told Chauncey he'd be sure to get sick some day and then he'd be sorry he hadn't made the pants. It was the only time I'd heard him make reference to being a doctor. I figured Chauncey must really be a good friend.

To be sure I needed new clothes. I'd grown a lot that year and both my pant legs and sleeves were too short. My shirts were too tight across the shoulders. My father said it was as much the work I was doing as it was the growing that made my clothes tight.

It was strange seeing my father sitting empty-handed and relaxed in the stern while Chauncey rowed. It was great to smell the water again and be right out on it in the breeze. I wished I had my own boat. I wanted one more than anything. I wished I could do some of the rowing. I had so much energy. I wanted something to push against. I'd have asked my father, but I didn't feel comfortable asking Chauncey.

I could tell Sammy was enjoying being on the water again too.Instead of curling up in the bottom he put his paws up on the gunwale and let his ears flap in the breeze.

When we got home the cabin looked okay, pretty much the way we left it except without the snow. Chauncey pulled up his boat. He was coming up for a bottle of maple syrup. "Hey, Chaunce," my father said, "You've got too many boats over there at your place. You don't need that many, just one man. You can only row one at a time."

"I need extras for my guests. Sometimes they like to just rent a boat from me rather than hire a guide."

"You've got two canoes. How many of the sportsmen rent canoes?"

"The women like them, they like to see where they're going, and they're smaller, easier for them to lift out of the water."

"How many women do you get coming through there at one time? I think you should sell me one of your canoes."

"Don't know, maybe. It'll cost you."

My father grinned. "Think about it," he said. Chauncey was climbing into his boat. "We'll come by in about a week to pick it up."

"I'll think about it but don't expect anything. I like a canoe now and then. They're handy for some things."

We watched him for a minute until he was out of earshot then my father said, "Well, if Chauncey doesn't sell us one of his, we'll try Long Lake, some of the boat builders up there. Somebody ought to have one they don't need."

I just couldn't figure my father out. Sometimes it seemed like he didn't care what happened to me or what I wanted and other times he was three steps ahead of me and ready with what I had just begun to yearn for.

As it turned out it wasn't too hard to talk Chauncey out of his smallest boat; a little blue canoe, ten feet long and two paddles. My father wouldn't tell me what he paid for it. It was my birthday present he said, a bit early.

It was much slower than a guide boat, but it gave me my freedom and I thought it was a wonderful little boat.

We'd left home in a hurry so we had some tidying up to do. We also had some syrup that we needed to boil down into sugar. We hadn't any meat so I used that as an excuse to go fishing. I enjoyed being out in my own boat alone.

After my father finished the sugar and got all the winter stuff cleaned and put away he got us going on the garden. "Got to get it all ready for planting before the black flies hatch," he said. He handed me a shovel and we began turning under the leaves we'd put on in the fall. It was early May and we had a few weeks before we could plant most things, but we got the soil ready.

I wondered why he was so concerned about the black flies. He'd pointed them out to me in the summer, but they were small and nowhere near as annoying as the mosquitoes. My father had told stories about them to the sportsmen, in the evening around the campfire. But I stopped taking those seriously early in the summer. They were exaggerations for entertainment or to impress the people who would believe anything.

But the flies truly were horrible and they came almost overnight. It was early June and we had already planted the peas and the potatoes. We were starting to plant the squash and beans and root vegetables. It was about nine o'clock in the morning and really warming up. They started to land, three or four on my head at a time. I felt little stings as they bit. They seemed to like my eyes, ears and scalp best.

My father looked up from planting carrots and I could see the surprised look on his face. "I haven't been bitten once but you've got blood trickling down both sides of your face," he said.

I put my hand up to my cheek and it came away with a smear of blood on it. I was surprised too. They'd been annoying, but I hadn't noticed the blood.

"You'd better go inside now," my father said. "Wash yourself up a bit then read a book or take a nap. Stay inside for the rest of the day."

"I can just put some bug repellent on," I said. "We've still got some left over from last year."

"Won't do much good. You stay inside. Go on now."

I went in and Sammy went with me.I thought they were both acting strange. Last year I complained bitterly about the mosquitoes and my father only laughed. By the time I found his shaving mirror I was feeling kind of tight around my left eye and my bites were beginning to really itch. I could feel blood caked in my hair.

What I saw in the mirror was awful. My eye was swollen almost shut and there was a streak of blood down the left side of my face and a smear on the right side where I'd put my hand.

I stuck my head in the wash basin and lathered it up good with soap. The cold water felt good on the itching bites, but by the time I rinsed off the soap I was feeling dizzy. I went in to my father's room and lay down on his bed.

It wasn't long before I heard my father come stamping in. He sounded like he had been running. He came in the room and blood was running down his face too.

"They're too much for me," he said. "I'll have to finish planting in the early morning before it warms up. Your eye looks pretty bad. How are you feeling?"

"Hot, dizzy, and a little sick."

"They got to you before they did me. If I'd known I'd have sent you in sooner. They like new blood. Guess I'll have to go back out again."

I wondered why, but he was out of the room before I had my wits about me enough to ask. Soon I saw him moving around outside. He was dressed in his winter hat and boots with a scarf tied around his neck and another around the lower part of the face--like a bandit. He was picking something off the ground. The amazing thing was that there was what looked like a black smudge all around his head the flies were so thick.

I lay back down wondering how long the flies would be like this and if I would have to go through this every year.

My father came back in and I could hear him puttering around in the next room. It sounded like he was chopping something. I dozed off and when I woke up he was daubing something warm and green onto my face.

"What is it?" I said.

"Plantain. It ought to soothe you some, take down the swelling. There are other things that would work but plantain is close at hand and to tell you the truth I don't like being out long when they're like this. The bites don't bother me much anymore, it's just that constant buzzing in your eyes and nose and mouth. It's enough to drive a person crazy."

"Why weren't they like this last year?"

"You came too late. They're only bad until it starts to heat up and dry out some. Then they lose their punch."

My father got the garden planted working the next two mornings, early, before the sun warmed off the chill.

I stayed inside feeling pretty sick. It's hard to know if my father's poultice helped because I don't know how I would have felt without it.

The third day he said he was tired of being forced inside, we were going fishing. He assured me we could outrun the flies easily in his boat. He was right. We spent the better part of the next two weeks out on the water, fishing and reading or just talking about this and that.

My father liked to tell stories. Sometimes I thought he must have gone into guiding so he would have an audience. I wondered how he'd gotten along all those winters without someone to talk to. That's not to say he didn't go long spells without saying something, but often he'd talk for hours. Sometimes it aggravated me that we couldn't just do something without him explaining all about it. We'd cut down a tree and he had to explain how the sap flows and why the tree needs its leaves. We dressed a deer and he pointed out where the food goes after it's swallowed. We cut up the deer and he explained to me about tendons and muscles. Often he repeated himself.

Those days we spent dodging the black flies he was thinking and talking about history, wars in particular. He started with the Peloponnesian wars and ended up with the American war for independence. I was waiting for him to get to the War Between the States. I wanted to hear stories about things that had happened to him then. But he didn't mention it.

I said, "Didn't you meet Charlie in the War?" He sat quietly for a minute, frowning, then he said, "That was a dirty war. Men fighting their own people. And disease killed more than the fighting did." He stopped a minute to reel in his line. "But I guess if you're not looking at them from the distance of history all wars are dirty."

Then he started in on the Constitution. I realized

that it was going to take a lot more than a suggestion to get him to talk about his war experiences.

CHAPTER TWELVE

I turned eleven at home. No party with strangers like last year, just my father and me. I knew my canoe was my birthday present and I wasn't expecting anything else, but there was a large package from Uncle John. My father had picked it up in Long Lake on his last trip there. Clothes. I never thought I would be so excited about getting clothes. It was wonderful to be able to move freely again. I also got some ammunition.

Eleven seemed so old compared to ten. I felt like a different person. When I thought of how little I knew just one year before it made me embarrassed.

My father didn't take me with him as often on his guiding trips as he had the past year. I couldn't keep up with him in my slow little canoe and I couldn't lift and carry it from one lake to another. Usually I knew when he would be on Raquette Lake. I took him berries and fresh stuff from the garden, spent the night, then went out fishing with him and his patrons the next day. If I didn't like the people he was working for I left. I was free to go wherever I wanted and do whatever I wanted. My only duty was weeding the garden.

I spent a lot of time exploring the new buildings going up. A man named Stott was building a place on Bluff point. He had several children, but they were all girls. Charlie Bennett had moved from Long Point to Constable Point and was building a big hotel. But it was the Durant place that fascinated me the most.

By then Mr. William West Durant must have noticed me. I hovered around a lot, just offshore.But he never gave me any notice. I couldn't stay away. He was building a regular estate, and the houses reminded me of Swiss Chalet.

Of course Mr. Durant was not doing the building himself. He'd brought in quite a few people to do the work. They drew me there as much as the building.

There were even women to cook and clean. One of the carpenters had a wife and son with him. The wife cooked and the son ran around and fetched things for his father or mother as he was needed or mostly if he was within earshot.

I spotted the boy early in the summer. He looked to be around my age, and I tried to find a way to make his acquaintance without actually trespassing. It was in mid July when I spotted him poking around alone in the woods along the south shore of the point. I paddled in and he grabbed the bow of the canoe and got in. "This boat yours?" he asked. I said it was and felt a flush of pride and knew at once I had something to offer.

Ned Tilson was twelve and was fascinated by boats. But he'd never rowed or paddled one himself. I gave him a lesson and let him go at it. From then until the weather turned cold I spent a lot of time with Ned. Except for his parents the adults paid little notice of me. I might have been part of the crew. Often I even ate there.

Ned wasn't nearly as educated as I was, but he taught me a lot about building and woodworking. One of his jobs, when he was around to do it, was to keep track of the tools and get the ones his father needed. He showed me what they were used for. Sometimes we hung around watching the men work. Sometimes we ran off into the woods. Ned taught me some things about the different kinds of trees that my father hadn't mentioned, things woodworkers need to know, about grain and color and hardness of the wood.

He told me he was going to be a carpenter himself. We built a fort up in an old pine tree. That's where we went when we didn't feel like doing anything but talk. That's where we were when I told Ned I was going to be a doctor.

"A doctor! Why on this earth would you want to do that?" He sounded scandalized.

"Doctors know a lot. They heal people and everybody looks up to them."

Ned snorted. "Doctors can't do nothing. I had a sister once. She swallowed a nail and my pa went and got the doctor, but he couldn't do a thing for her. She died soon enough. My aunt had consumption and she went to a whole bunch of doctors, but she died, too. They don't know much. What you should do is become a carpenter like me. Everybody wants houses built."

I was pretty insulted to hear him talk that way. I'd promised my father I wouldn't blab about him, so I couldn't tell Ned about Jock's leg. I wouldn't ever tell him about my mother. But I figured being a doctor ran in my family just like being a carpenter ran in his. I just said, "Doctors fix broken bones and keep people from dying of gangrene."

"That ain't much. Besides, where you ever goin' to get the schooling for that? You're only eleven and you don't go to school no more. Even I go to school."

He had me there. I didn't know where I'd get my schooling. I just said, "I'll find a way."

Ned liked to look down on me a bit because I was a year younger than he was, and I wasn't planning on being a carpenter. But most of the time we had fun together. He liked my boat, and I taught him how to swim.

His parents were pretty easy on him, and we went out for three or four days at a time with nothing but some flour and bacon. We took fishing line and my gun and usually got along just fine. We could do the carries with both of us under the boat.

It would be pretty hard to starve in the summer. Most of July there are raspberries. Then at the end of the month the blueberries start ripening and last into the first part of August. About that time the shadberries become edible, then the chokecherries. If you wait long enough you can always get a fish. We spent a lot of time fishing and picking berries but hardly ever in the same place twice.

We came to no harm. Our biggest close call came when we pulled the canoe up on the sand and went inland to hunt for berries. The trouble was, we didn't pull the boat up far enough. When we got back a bit of wind had kicked up and the waves had lifted the boat and floated it out somewhere. We were on an island and everything we had with us was in the canoe.

Ned was furious. "How could you have let that happen, we'll never get off this island."

"Hey, wait a minute," I said. "You were the last one out of the boat. You let me off to scout out if it was a berry island. When I hollered you pulled it up and joined me."

His face went red and he said, "Oh, yeah," very quietly.

"We'd better concentrate on finding the canoe," I said. I'm afraid it's going to be bashed up against the rocks."

We split up and walked around the shore looking out for it and had almost come together again on the other side when we saw it. It was moving slowly toward the middle of the lake. I didn't know how far I could swim, but I knew it was moving away from us, and if I wanted to reach my boat I would have to start swimming right away. I stripped my clothes off and jumped in.

I was not a fast swimmer, but I had stamina. I reached my canoe with enough energy left to lift myself up over the stern. I knew better than to try climbing over the side. I'd done that once earlier in the summer when I was alone. It filled with water and I had to pull it to shore to empty it. It's a whole lot easier pulling an empty canoe than a full one.

When I picked up Ned he said, "I'm really sorry, Will. I'll never do that again. I promise."

"That's OK," I said. "Just don't be so quick to blame me." That was the only thing I didn't like about

Ned. He liked to treat me like a little kid whenever he could.

Mr. Durant built a dam on the Marion River at the west end of Utowana. It was to raise the level of Eagle and Utowana Lakes just enough so a large boat could get through from Blue Mt. Lake to the carry. Ned and I had been up there a couple of times to watch the work.

Durant put a small steamboat named the Utowana on the lakes so the people staying at hotels in Blue could ride the boat to the end of Utowana Lake. Ned and I paddled up the Marion the day it was supposed to take its first trip. We walked the carry path to the end of the lake to watch the steamboat land. There was a big, sturdy wooden landing there. People could disembark and walk around. It was very grand and exciting to watch the boat come chugging down the lake toward us. Compared to the guide boats and canoes we were in every day it seemed like a huge thing. I held my breath watching it land, wondering if it would stop soon enough or if it would smash into the landing. But it glided alongside slowly and someone I didn't know jumped off with a rope. Eighteen people got off, four of them ladies in very fancy dress. The people acted like they'd just done something very important. I felt like saying, "I got here before you."

Ned wanted to ride on it, but we didn't have money. Worse than that, we didn't have a way back. I felt bad for Ned, but I wasn't sure how I felt about the steam boat. If Durant put one on Raquette Lake would it put my father and the other guides out of business?

Ned left in September, but he thought he would be back next year. I missed him a lot. My main disappointment with him was, I couldn't get anything out of him about school. I desperately wanted to know what boys my age were learning. I didn't want to get too far behind. How would I ever get into medical school? I pictured myself sitting in sixth grade at the age of eighteen, seventh grade at nineteen, etc. At that rate I would be twenty-four before I'd be ready to even take the exams. But when I pressed him on what he learned at school Ned only said, "Oh just the same old stuff."

With Ned gone I spent more time with my father. We dug the potatoes, took in the squash and carried leaves like we had the year before. But I enjoyed it more this time. We hunted and stocked up on wood. The water became too cold for swimming.

We were confined to the house one cold, drizzly October day. I was trying to whittle a beaver out of a piece of pine and my father was mending his snowshoes. "How would you like to have a mother, Will?" he said suddenly.

"I thought he was really asking because he wanted to know so I said, "I don't think I'd like it much now. I've gotten used to going where ever I want. A mother would probably want me to stay around so she'd know where I was."

My father chuckled. "Well now, Will, I don't think it will be that bad."

"What do you mean?" I said. I was feeling uneasy and beginning to get the idea that he wasn't just asking me for something to talk about.

"I'm getting married, Will, to an old friend of yours, Elizabeth Grayson. I asked her this summer when I was guiding her and her folks. Next June we'll go to Albany and have the wedding. You'll stay with the Graysons for a week while Elizabeth and I go on our honeymoon. The Graysons and I arranged it all the last part of their stay this summer, after I proposed to her."

My first thought was, "Why didn't he ask me first. Just when I'm enjoying my life he has to go and change things." But as soon as I thought it I knew it was unreasonable. Adults didn't ask young people for permission. They made the decisions and we had to go along. But I was glad it was Elizabeth. I thought she was okay.

When the first shock was over I started thinking about how it might be nice to have a mother for once. It would be nice to have someone there in the house when my father was gone, especially when he was off on a drunk. Then I wondered if she knew about that. Probably not. She never saw him in the winter. He never drank in the summer. I wondered if I should tell her. Maybe she wouldn't believe me. Maybe she would believe me and not marry him. That's when I decided I really wanted my father to marry Elizabeth Grayson.

The colder the weather got the more I looked forward to having someone else in the house. Then the ice froze and we set our traps. We had a longer trap line this year because I knew what I was doing and we could each take care of half the traps without my father having to check mine. We still went up the brooks to Shallow Lake, only my father went further up Sucker Brook. My line went up Beaver Brook then down into Pelcher pond.

On days at home we had plenty to do. My father was making snowshoes, mittens and slippers for Elizabeth as well as the things we needed for ourselves.

I did my father's trap line four times that winter, three because he was out drinking with Chauncey and once when he had to go to Blue to set a broken leg.

CHAPTER THIRTEEN

It was spring again and I was excited for the change. We hung up our traps and brought out the sap buckets. We waited for the ice to go out and placed bets on when it would be. We had to be able to paddle out between our house and Kenwell's point and have clear water as far north and south as we could see. The stakes were this: If I won, we got to ride the stage to North Creek on our way to the wedding. If my father won we walked.

The break up was more dramatic at our house than it had been at Thirtyfour Flow. It must have been because the lake was so much bigger. The ice heaved up cracking and roaring onto the rocks along the shore. We stood up the hill just far enough to be out of the way and watched ice cakes float north. When it looked clear enough to check it out with the boat we had to work for two hours, pushing the ice out of the way with poles to make a path to the water. The pile of ice that had heaved up was higher than my father's head and the chunks were a good two feet thick.As before, it was a real thrill to be out on the open water again. This time we were in my boat and I got to paddle.

It was the nineteenth of April. I had guessed the fifteenth and my father guessed the twentieth, meaning we would be walking to North Creek and would have to start earlier. But as it turned out we took the stage anyway. Cool weather held out until the tenth of June. We had the garden in and still no black flies. They came on strong two days before we left. Even my father wouldn't walk to North Creek while the flies were bad so we rowed to Blue and shut ourselves inside the stage.

It was almost two years since I'd been out of the woods. I was excited to ride the train and see the city again. Even Albany would seem huge after living on Raquette Lake. I had money and spent a long time pondering what I would spend it on.

My father was excited, too. I could tell by the way he talked--faster than usual.

The stage trip was truly awful. I told my father I wished he had been able to keep his part of the bet. My bottom and shoulder blades were bruised and I had a lump on my head by the time we reached North Creek.

We ate on the train, slept some then changed into the best clothes we had. The Graysons were there to meet us when we got to Albany.

Their house was at least as grand as my grandparent's home in London. I had a room to myself. Behind the main house were stables. They had horses for pulling their coach and horses just to ride. When Mr. Grayson found out I had never ridden he promised to give me lessons while my father and Elizabeth were gone.

I wondered if my father had known before that the Graysons were this rich. I wondered if they realized how poor we were and just how Elizabeth would be living when she moved to the lake. It didn't mean anything to my father. He'd been this rich growing up too. I decided I had to tell Elizabeth about my father. It was only fair.

My chance came the day before the wedding when he was out getting his clothes fitted. I found her in the garden, sitting on a bench. I went over and asked if I might sit down and talk to her. She said "Certainly William." There was something about the way she said it that made me feel a little squirmy. When I'd been with her last summer and the summer before she'd acted straightforward and chummy. Now it seemed like she was trying to be sweet and motherly. I started to feel really nervous in the pit of my stomach. This was not a good time to be telling her these things, but I didn't have any choice.

"Elizabeth," I said. "I just want to tell you I'm really glad you're marrying Dad."

"Why thank you, William. I'm looking forward to having you for a son."

"I think we'll get along all right," I said. "I just want to warn you about the winters. They are awfully lonesome and cold. The lake is different when it has ice and snow on it. Dad's different, too, in the winter time. He drinks."

Elizabeth was losing her motherly look. She stared at me for a few minutes with an expression that changed from uncertain and worried to suspicious. "All men drink a bit, William."

"My father leaves for 3 or 4 days at a time without warning. It's real lonesome, and I never know when he's coming back. It's not so bad once you get used to it, but the first couple of times it's scary and I just wanted to warn you before it happens.

"Is there anything else you want to warn me about, William?" She wasn't sounding sweet anymore.

"Yes, I guess I might as well tell you about the flies. They're really bad in June. When we get back we might have to spend a couple of weeks inside. Even Dad doesn't do much outside when the black flies are bad. And, I also wanted to tell you that when you grow up rich like you and I did it's kind of hard to get used to all the work.

"I'm very used to work William. I have been working for five years. I am an independent woman, and I have never been lazy."

"Well, I guess I'll go read now," I said. I got out of her sight as soon as I could. I could tell she thought I just didn't want her to marry Dad. I hoped she wouldn't tell him what I said, and I also hoped she wouldn't hold it against me after we got back home. But at least when it all happened she couldn't blame me for not telling her.

That evening at supper she was very quiet. My father had just come back from his fitting, and he was doing most of the talking. I tried not to look right at her.

I figured she was really mad at me and I wondered how it would be living with her if she stayed mad. The meal was served. They had a cook. I wondered if Elizabeth knew how to cook venison and cornbread. I hoped she liked squash.

The wedding was pretty fancy with lots of delicate foods afterward. What impressed me the most was seeing my father in those clothes. He didn't look like himself.But the biggest surprise I had was seeing my Uncle John and Aunt Hope there. I was sort of shocked really. I thought he would be upset by the marriage because his sister had been my father's first wife. But then I remembered that he and the Graysons were friends before they ever met my father. My mother had been dead for almost twelve years. I supposed it was all right for my father to get married again.

My uncle sat down next to me at the reception and asked me how everything had gone since I'd moved in with my father. He didn't seem as uncomfortable talking to me as I remembered.

"I'm all right," I said. "I wish I could go to school. But besides that I'm liking it fine." That was all I needed to say. That was the polite thing to say. But I had had so many imaginary conversations with my uncle the past two years that I just blurted out; "Why didn't you tell me about my father? Why did you let me go all the way from London to Indian Lake thinking he would kill me when you could have told me what he was like?" I could feel my face getting hot. That was a very impertinent way to behave toward an adult I hardly knew.

"I'm sorry, Will," he said. "I didn't think you would listen to me. Your grandparents had thoroughly prejudiced you and I was merely a stranger. You were very hostile you know."

That surprised me. I had never thought of myself as hostile.

"But they told me he killed my mother. I thought

he was illiterate. Perhaps if someone had just told me he was a doctor or even that he was educated."

"Perhaps," my uncle said. But he sounded very doubtful.

I had brought up the doctor subject and that made me think of another question I had been wanting to ask someone besides my father. "Uncle John," I said, "may I ask you a very important question?"

I thought he hesitated a bit but he cleared his throat and said, "Certainly."

"What's the real reason my grandparents called another doctor when I was being born?"

He took a deep breath then looked at the floor a moment before he turned to me and said, "What do you think William? After two years haven't you made any guesses on that one.?"

"Was he drinking?"

He looked relieved, perhaps that I had said it, and he hadn't had to. "Yes, of course, William."

"So you think it was his fault? If he hadn't been drinking my mother would still be alive."

"No one knows the answer to that. All I know is, drunk or sober, your father would never have forgotten to wash his hands."

I almost laughed because it was so true, and it was a relief to know my uncle wasn't blaming him. I would have liked to ask him more about my mother and my father, but Aunt Hope came and sat down with us.

The next day Elizabeth and my father went on their honeymoon and I was left with the Graysons.

Mr. Grayson said I was a natural on a horse. I didn't feel like a natural, especially the third day when I woke up so stiff in the legs that I had to slide down the stairs on my bottom. He said the same thing my father said when I first went to the mountains. "The best thing to do is just keep on doing it. The exercise works the soreness out."

So we rode a lot down through their back meadow and through the woods to the Hudson River. I could tell Mr. Grayson loved to ride by the amount of time we spent at it. He was not spending time with me out of duty and that made me feel comfortable. I rode a young mare named Nutmeg, and she seemed to like me.

One day I asked him if he didn't mind his daughter marrying a poor man from the woods instead of a rich one nearby. He laughed and said it gave him an excuse to go into the mountains more often. "Also," he said, "Elizabeth is a pretty outspoken woman. Not many men can put up with that. She's twenty four and I was afraid I'd never have any grandchildren. I think your father is just right for her. Besides, I get a grandson without even having to wait."

That surprised me and gave me something new to think about. I hadn't considered how this might change my life except for having a mother. Now I had grand-parents again. Maybe I would be coming here fairly often.

Suddenly I had a thought. "How much would it cost me to get to England?" I asked him. He told me and I laughed.

"What's this all about," he said.

"I was just thinking that two years ago all I could think of was getting back to England. I plotted and schemed about how I would get enough money, so I could run away from my father and escape. I've got enough money right now, but I don't want to do that anymore."

Mr. Grayson laughed. "Well, I should hope not. We'd all miss you."

Elizabeth and my father must have had a good time because they were both smiling and comfortable when they got back from their trip. She treated me like she used to and seemed to have forgotten our talk the week before. We stayed two more days then went home. Mrs.

Grayson cried at the station and Elizabeth reminded her that it would only be a few weeks until they were visiting us at the lake.

We had to take the stage this time, flies or no flies, because we had so much baggage. Besides Elizabeth's trunks we had books both my father and I had bought and some of my things that had been left with Uncle John.

My father's guide boat was at Blue, of course, but he put Elizabeth and me and our baggage on the Utowana. It was great fun riding on that steamboat. I thought of how I would be able to tell Ned about it. The most fun though, was watching my father race it. It took the Utowana some time to get up speed. It didn't take my father long at all. He reached the passage between Blue and Eagle long before we did. We gained on him on the lake, but he still went into Utowana ahead of us. We passed him in the middle of Utowana but he never fell far behind.

We put all our baggage on the landing and the Utowana left us. The flies were still bad. We opened our bags and found things to wrap around our heads. We put socks on our hands. Our eyes were still exposed and the little bugs often managed to crawl under our wrappings.

Dad carried the boat and Elizabeth and I carried a bag in each hand. She already had blood around her eyes and I felt bad for her. We'd probably both be down sick for the next few days. The path was 3/4 of a mile long and it seemed to take us forever to walk it, we stopped so often to hold our hands over our faces just to get some relief from the buzzing.

My father passed us on his way back for some baggage then he passed us again going back with it. He was loading a box of books when we got to the boat. "We're better off leaving the clothes and taking the books," he said. "The clothes can handle getting wet if it rains. I won't go back for any more right now. We've got to get Elizabeth out of these flies. It's going to be a bad trip down the Marion as it is."

I had forgotten about that. With all the twists of the river it was impossible to go fast and the flies buzzed us constantly until we were out on open water. Elizabeth sat in the bow with her head buried in her arms and I sat in the stern, doing my best to steer us around the bends. She must be starting to feel pretty sick by now I thought and I wondered why I wasn't. I was swollen though and having a hard time seeing.

When we got home we were almost frantic to get into the house. My father washed Elizabeth's face and made a poultice. He told me to put some on myself. Then he went out again to get more of our stuff. I thought of him having to go all the way up and down the river again and making probably 2 or 3 trips on the path to carry the stuff. "Do you want me to go with you?" I asked. "It will go faster if I'm there to steer and help carry things."

He thought about that a moment then said, "No. I think I can get everything in the boat if you aren't with me. It will be full but it's a calm day. I'll be all right."

I was tremendously relieved. I checked on Elizabeth. She was very swollen but asleep. I daubed some of the green mash on my eyes and took out one of my new books. I itched like crazy and my face was tight but I was okay.

I checked the lake often to see if the wind was picking up. I figured if the lake got rough I could go out to meet my father in my canoe and take part of his load. But the evening stayed calm. I made a batch of biscuits and when I saw my father's boat cut across the path of the moon on the water I put some bacon and potatoes on to fry. I went down to help him with the baggage.

We unloaded the boat and he lifted it out of the water and put it upside down on the shore. He asked me to sit down a minute. I sat on a rock. "Son, I want you to be nice to Elizabeth."

"Of course. I was planning on it. Why wouldn't I be nice to her?" I wondered if she had told him about our talk.

"It's just that we're used to living alone here and doing pretty much what we please. She's going to have different ideas about how to run a house. She's going to feel like she has to be a good wife and mother and until we get things all figured out our ideas will probably clash a bit. She's had a rough start already. It hasn't been quite what she expected. I want you to try and remember how it was when you first came. There was a lot you didn't know." He paused a bit. "I suspect there will be a few things she won't know how to do and it will frustrate her. Just try not to laugh at her or get impatient, all right."

"I understand Dad. I already figured I'd do the cooking for a while."

"Good. And remember, she probably will try to put restrictions on you you're not used to. Don't get upset. Just let me handle it."

"I'll try."

Things didn't work out quite the way we planned and that was because of Elizabeth's own nature. She didn't get sick from her bites like I had. She just itched a lot and went frantic from the buzzing whenever she went outside. My father took her out fishing and explained that that was about all we could do right now, read and fish and putter around the house. But the third day I was by the stove getting ready to make supper and she snatched the pan out of my hands.

"Here," she said. "Let me do the cooking. All you ever make is bacon, beans, fish, cornbread, and potatoes."

I didn't know what to say, so I just backed off and decided I'd let my father deal with it. She rummaged around in the cupboard then went out back to the shed. When she came back in she stood in the middle of the room with her hands on her hips and said, "Benson Chadwick, there is nothing in this place to eat except bacon, flour, cornmeal and potatoes, oh yes, and navy beans."

"There's one squash left, up in my bedroom," I offered.

"We've planted the garden," my father said. "In about a month we should have lettuce. In two months we'll have peas and green beans, beets, turnips and carrots."

Her face began to sort of crumble and I wondered whether she was going to get mad or cry.

"I could go to Long Lake. Someone might sell me a chicken. I'm sure I could find some cheese or butter. I could go shoot a rabbit or some venison. As for vegetables and fruit my dear, I'm afraid you're just going to have to wait."

She went into the bedroom and my father and I went back to what we were doing. I felt terribly sorry for her, but I couldn't do anything about it. I figured she was in there crying. But not five minutes later she strode back into the room and grabbed the knife from me that I was using to slice potatoes.

"I've got to have something to do around here," she said, "or I'll go crazy."

I watched her. She didn't know that to make biscuits you had to put in baking powder and grease. She put everything on the stove at the same time, so the potatoes were still hard and the fish were black and falling apart. The biscuits were just hard chunks of flour, water and salt not quite done in the middle.

We ate very quietly. We were all having a hard time getting it down. finally my father said, "My dear, I admire your willingness to try something you've never done before."

"I can make cakes," she snapped. "I've made lots of cakes. But you can't make a cake without eggs and lard."

We were all silent a bit longer than she said. "Why are my biscuits so flat and hard."

"You have to put baking powder in them to make them rise and fat to soften them up a bit. We pour bacon grease into them."

"But I never saw you use baking powder when we were out camping."

"I mix it into the flour before I pack it. It's more convenient on guiding trips."

"Oh, I see. How do I know when to start the fish so that it all gets done at the same time?"

"When the potatoes don't feel crunchy anymore when you poke them. It's the same with venison if it's sliced thin."

"All right. I don't want to eat another meal like this any more than you do."

I had to admire her. She must have been really embarrassed, but she made the best of it.

The next morning my father set off in his boat without saying a word to either of us about where he was going. He headed north. I worried a little, but he was back before dark with two chickens, a large tin of lard and a bunch of dandelion greens. There was also a large sack of feed for the chickens. "I talked somebody out of two of their laying hens," he said. They ought to give us two eggs a day. Tomorrow Will and I will make them a pen."

I hate dandelion greens. They're bitter and tough, but Elizabeth ate them without complaining.

CHAPTER FOURTEEN

Elizabeth tried really hard to become a good cook, and she did fine. There wasn't a whole lot of variety, and that frustrated her. The eggs helped. There were times, she told me, when she yearned for a nice loaf of yeast bread.

There were worse things than the cooking that had to be figured out. The biggest problem was me going off alone in my canoe any old place and not coming back for two or three days at a time. She said a twelve-year-old had no place doing such things. I could get lost or drown or break a leg and no one would ever find me.

By then I was used to being on my own and I was shocked that anyone would object to it. I couldn't see how I would be able to confine myself the way she wanted me to. My father came to my rescue, but they had a good-sized argument about it. I got to keep my freedom, but my father reminded me that with him guiding and me off rambling, Elizabeth was alone and stuck.

After that I took her out with me more. We fished and picked berries. Often I took her across to visit Olive Kenwell who was about the same age as Elizabeth. Sometimes I took her to Blanchard's where she helped Hattie with her children and her work. It put restrictions on me because I had to be back in the evening to take her home.

Ned's father was keeping him around more. Ned was thirteen and it was time for him to start learning his trade. At least three days of the week he was expected to help with the work. I hung around and watched and fetched the tools they needed. I was pleased with myself that I knew enough to be able to do that. As I watched the buildings take shape I thought that carpentry wouldn't be a bad job if I wasn't going to be a doctor.

One day I confided to Elizabeth that I wanted to be

a doctor, but I was afraid I was getting hopelessly behind in school.

"Will, don't you remember that I have been teaching school for several years? I will be glad to help you catch up to your grade level. We can get to work on it as soon as the summer is over. Another thing, don't tell your father I told you this, but my parents have offered to have you go live with them. You could go to a good school down there. Would you like to do that?"

"Like it? I think it is a great idea. I won't have to wait until I'm twenty-four to finish school."

I began dreaming about living in Albany, riding Nutmeg in the afternoons and studying in the evening. I wouldn't have to go trapping anymore. That was one thing I hadn't learned to like. I still hated trapping.

The weather began to turn cold. Ned left and my father was guiding less often. We got in the vegetables. But there was no mention of me going anywhere. Elizabeth set up studies for me like we were in a school room. My last schooling was when I was nine, so I had three years to catch up on. After three weeks Elizabeth said I was ahead of my age level in everything but spelling and art. She taught me perspective and color and drilled me in spelling then decided she would teach me French. My father laughed at our formal lessons but suggested she teach me Latin. I could tell it was not one of her favorites, but I did learn some basics along with the French. It was fun to have something to study again, but I was puzzled that I should be ahead after three years. I came to the conclusion that American Schools must be run much differently than the English schools.

We started our trap lines and my formal instruction was wedged in between trips to Shallow Lake. Then early December my father went off on a drunk. Elizabeth was expecting a baby and I was glad she didn't have to be all alone and wondering what was going on like I had my first time.

She didn't catch on to what was happening at first. She was very worried something had happened to him. I didn't want to bring it up because I was still embarrassed about that talk I had with her before they were married. I had to go run the trap line--my half and his half. It was a good clear day and the snow was firm, so I told her I would try to be back not long after dark. I did it but I was up half the night skinning and stretching the hides. She stayed up with me. I guessed she'd been crying because her eyes were red and puffy.

I mostly tried to keep my mouth shut, but I couldn't help telling her not to worry, he'd be back in a day or two and he'd be just fine.

"You tried to warn me and I wasn't very nice to you about it, was I? Let's see, you warned me about the flies, the loneliness in the winter and the drinking and work. I like the work, but you were right about everything else." She frowned. "This just doesn't seem to fit his personality."

He came back the next day just before dark. He was drunk and talking about everything he could think of as usual. But Elizabeth didn't deal with the situation the way I had. She was mad and she wasn't afraid to say just what she thought. I got out of there and went to bed but I could hear her going on to him about having a baby and being left alone with a twelve-year-old boy. She was wasting her time. The next day he wouldn't remember a word of it.

After things quieted down and I couldn't hear anybody moving around I went down for something to eat. My father was curled up on the floor by the stove asleep. I put some wood on the fire and went back to bed.

He was fixing breakfast when I got up. He was good-natured as usual. I gave him my report on the trapping, and he said he'd seen the pelts in the shed.

I wondered what Elizabeth would do the next time. But there wasn't a next time that winter.

Three days later we came back with our catch. My father was out back splitting wood and I was on the porch skinning a muskrat when I heard him holler. It was a wordless yell, but there was something in it that made me jump and run. Elizabeth got there first, running out the back door ahead of me.

He was lying on the ground. I think he had passed out for a moment. The axe was lying by his leg. Blood covered the snow. He looked down at his leg from where he lay. "Cut the pants away Will and we'll see what we've got to deal with". I could hear the doctor in his voice taking over.

I still had my skinning knife in my hand and I sliced the pant leg away. I felt a little sick when the flesh rolled back a bit and I saw bone. Blood was oozing out but not gushing. I looked up at Elizabeth who was white and gripping her skirt. "We'd better go in and wash our hands," I said. "Boil everything in my bag," my father said, then he closed his eyes. "And bring me some whisky."

We ran into the house together. I hauled his doctor's bag out of the little closet where he kept it and started putting the instruments into the pot Elizabeth was filling from the water pail. I couldn't see how we would need them all but I knew better than to try to pick and choose.

"We don't have any whiskey," I said, "what was he talking about?"

"Yes, we do. It's in the closet in our bedroom. I'll get it."

She hurried in there and brought it out.

"Here, you take it to him. I'll get the fire hot so this water boils."

I took it from her. "Has this always been here?"

"As long as we've been married at least. It sits on the shelf in back, behind some books. I asked him about it last summer and he said it was for medicinal purposes."

"He never drinks here," I said. "I'd know if he did, but he never has."

"I don't understand either Will. The man is a mystery. I guess we should just be glad he doesn't drink all the time."

I grabbed the bottle and went out with it.

He took a couple of big gulps. "That will numb me just a little. I think I'd better get inside. I'm starting to get cold. I don't want to stand up. See if you can drag me in."

I grabbed him by the shoulders and got him as far as the door step. I didn't want to drag him over that and didn't think I could anyway so I called Elizabeth. We got him inside near the stove. Elizabeth brought a blanket.

"Okay, Will, go back out and get the whiskey then pour some on my leg. When you've done that one of you will have to stitch me up. But I don't want you to do anything if I pass out. Wait until I wake up before you go on. Don't do anything if I'm out."

"All right Dad."

"Now who's going to do it?"

I looked at Elizabeth. I couldn't read much out of her expression, but she didn't look awfully eager. "I will," I said.

"All right, now pour the whiskey on."

I did it and he gritted his teeth, groaned and passed out. He came to quickly. "Always been one of my weak points, passing out." He said. "Is the horse hair in the pot, too?"

It was. I knew we would have to use that. Horsehair was what he used to sew people up. He took the long tail hairs. He said it was more natural to the human body than cotton. Skin healed better around it.

We had to wait for the water to boil, but my father used the time to give instructions. I had to put the sutures just so far apart. I had to slice off dead and mangled skin. The cut was about five inches long from his ankle up the leg along the shin bone. He kept raising himself up on his elbow to look at it. The blood was caked on by now and he had me throw a quantity of cotton rags into the water which was just beginning to boil. He kept saying how lucky he was that the cut wasn't an inch lower. "All those bones in the foot," he said. "I would never have walked normally again."

I was thinking about Jock and hoping desperately my father's leg wouldn't become gangrenous.

Stitching him up took a terribly long time. I was sore and cramped from my position on the floor. My stomach was churning from having to slice away at him. I tried to pretend I was just skinning an animal but it didn't help. It did help that I had skill with a knife.

Elizabeth had to help me hold the loose flap of skin in place. Twice she put her hand on the floor to steady herself and each time my father made her wash her hands before we went on. She seemed annoyed but I couldn't tell if it was with him or herself. Anyway, she stopped putting her hands down.

When I finished, Elizabeth helped him to the bed.

The cut healed well, and my father said I'd done a fine job of stitching him up. But the bone was bruised or maybe even broken. He cussed himself for not taking a better look at it, but when I asked him what he could have done about it he just grinned and said, "Nothing, but I'd know if it was safe to walk or not. Trouble is, it hurts to put weight on it and that's a sure sign I'd better stay off it."

I had to do all the work and was gone more than I was home. We had a deep, soft snowfall that made walking the trap line slow. I had to spend nights at the cabin on Shallow Lake no matter how fast I tried to go.

About a week after his accident I was home and my father said, "Will, I want you to teach Elizabeth to help you with the trap line. Take her with you like I did you at first then she can start doing half herself."

Elizabeth almost exploded. "I am expecting a baby."

"I know, and you're inside all day. You need more exercise."

"Exercise, I carry the water and wash the clothes. You don't think that's more exercise than I should be having in my condition?"

"No, I don't think it's enough. I know it's common for women to be pampered when they're in your condition, but I don't think it does them any good. It takes muscles to give birth, Elizabeth. The stronger the muscles the easier it is, just like any other work."

"I don't think we should be discussing such things around William," she said primly.

My father laughed. "Will, go busy yourself outside for awhile."

I left reluctantly. I could tell Elizabeth was mad, and I didn't want to be in the middle of an argument. But I could also tell by my father's tone of voice that he was about to launch into a lengthy explanation of the birth process and the muscles involved. It was a topic I had never heard or read about, and I was curious. It was one of those subjects no one talked about in polite company. I'd have to ask my father about it sometime when Elizabeth wasn't around.

I went down to the lake to fish.

It was a cold and windy day, and I was glad when Elizabeth called me up for lunch. I couldn't tell right away how the discussion had gone and didn't dare ask. The next morning, without saying a word about it, she pulled on her boots, coat and hat and followed me outside with her snowshoes under her arm.

"I guess now I'll find out about the work."

I could tell by the way she said it that she was not convinced it would be good for her.

She carried my father's packbasket. It was empty

except for extra socks and some potatoes, but she wanted to get used to carrying it.

Our progress was slow. Elizabeth had never done any real walking on her snowshoes, and she had to learn how to maneuver around and over things. I could see that her long skirts were not a help either. We found a muskrat on Beaver Brook and a fox on the cross over from the brook to Shallow Lake. The fox was still alive, just caught by the foot. I had to club it. Elizabeth cried. She said it reminded her of a small dog she had when she was a girl.

I couldn't blame her. When I came on an animal caught by the foot I always wondered if I should let it go or try to make a pet of it. My father said an injured animal wouldn't last long in the woods, and he also warned me that wild animals don't make good pets.

At the cabin she cooked up the potatoes and the meatiest parts of the muskrat while I skinned the fox. I felt bad because she was sad, and I wished she wasn't there to remind me of what it was like when I first started.

"I will come with you Will, if your father wants me to get exercise, but I will not do this by myself. I will not club animals to death. I don't even like to see them dead and think how long it took them to die. I wonder how long they had to be in pain. I will not do this alone. I'll walk to Blue and stay with Hattie Blanchard and ride out to the train on the mail sled. I will not do this."

She won on that one. My father sent us both to Long Lake for some supplies, so she would know the way. From then until the ice started to rot she walked to Long Lake every ten days, spent the night, then walked back. My father said it was good for her to have some female company, especially in her condition. "Women like to talk to one another about these things," he said. "It makes them feel better."

My father hobbled around the house, but his leg

didn't mend enough for any real walking until it was time to pull in the traps. He helped me with that, but it was slow work. By the time the ice went out he was back to normal except for a slight limp which stayed with him the rest of his life.

One day in early May my father sent me off in my canoe. He said he didn't care where I went but that I shouldn't come back for three days. I knew it was time for the baby to be born, so I wasn't offended, only pleased to be out on the water alone. It was almost a year since I'd had three whole days to be off by myself without work to do.

When I went back I had a sister, Clarissa. She was two days old.

CHAPTER FIFTEEN

Clarissa was puny and squirmy, and she completely changed our household. Elizabeth suddenly had much more work to do. What with all the washing and the feeding I carried water for her and started doing most of the cooking again.

The baby grew fast and became fat. After the flies died off that spring I took her out in the canoe with me often when I fished.

The house seemed full. Mrs. Grayson came the week after the baby was born and stayed two weeks. I had to give up my bed for her to use. She came again in July with Mr. Grayson and they stayed another two weeks. I was to call them Grandmother and Grandfather Grayson. She was bossy, so I stayed out of the way.

I spent a lot of time trying to pick up my canoe and carry it over my head. I could get under it and pick up one end then step backwards and pick up the other end and walk with it. But I couldn't pick it up out of the water and lift it over my head. I had to be able to do that before I could ever think of being a guide myself.

I knew of a sixteen-year-old who was working out of Old Forge. I hoped to be guiding myself the summer I turned fifteen. That was two more years. I had to grow, and I had to have a guide boat. This year my canoe seemed frustratingly slow.

Ned was fourteen and working full time with his father.He was even paid for it. He came out with me now and then, but he was serious about his work. I felt lonely and out of place. I was too old to do the same old things I'd been doing and too young to have any real work. When the Graysons left I found myself sticking around the house more to play with the baby and do jobs for Elizabeth. We spent some time on my French and Latin but I could tell her interest in it wasn't as strong as it had been.

"I talked to my father about your schooling, Will,"
she told me. "He is serious about having you down there
this winter to live with them. He said he had a talk with
your father about it."

"What did Dad say?"

"Nothing, but he seemed to be thinking about it."

This news got me so worked up I could think of
little else for days. I even went so far as to make a small
pile on my bedroom floor of the things I would want to
take with me. But my father never mentioned anything
to me about it until we were digging the potatoes that
fall.

"Have you met the Indian, Mitchell Sabattis?" he
asked.

I hadn't, but I had heard of him. He lived in Long
Lake and made guide boats.

"Well, I've been thinking that it's time you learned
something more than I've been teaching you. You need
to learn a trade, like Ned."

"I want to be a doctor," I said.

"Sure," he said, "but who ever heard of a thir-
teen-year-old doctor. You like working with wood, so
I've asked Sabattis if he'd take you on as an apprentice.
You'll spend the next few winters in Long Lake. I'll be
taking you up there in two weeks, so you had better be
thinking about what you want to take with you."

"But I thought I was going to Albany to go to
school. I know Grandfather Grayson talked to you about
it."

"Sure he did, Will, and he convinced me you
needed more to do, but you don't want to go to the city
yet. You'll be eight months away from home at a time.
Do you really want to be that confined? And think of
your sister. She'll be walking before you see her again.
She won't even remember you when you come back."

He had me there. He knew how attached I was to
the baby.

"You don't need to worry about becoming a doctor. You're only thirteen."

That was the end of the discussion. I was going to Long Lake and that was that, and to live with an Indian too. He'd probably get drunk some day and kill me. I'd been scared of Indians ever since I'd set foot in America. And seeing that Johnny in Moose's saloon hadn't helped.

I was angry all day and disappointed. Just because he doesn't like being a doctor, he thinks I shouldn't be one, I thought. He's trying to hold me to his way of thinking just like my grandparents tried to hold him to theirs. He wants to get me out of the house but still keep me under his control.

I went up to bed early that evening and looked bitterly at my little pile of books. What good would they do me now. I was going to be a boat builder the rest of my life.

Then a thought struck me. I had money. I wasn't sure how much things cost, but I knew I had enough to get to Albany. Maybe even to London. I might even have enough to enroll myself in boys school for a year if the Graysons wouldn't take me without my father's consent. I could go to any town between here and New York City and rent a room from someone and go to the public school. I had my own money.

This thought freed me up to think about Long Lake. They had a school there. Maybe I could go sometimes to find out what I was supposed to be learning and catch up on my own. I wouldn't be trapping this winter. I could make my own guideboat. I could get home once a week if I wanted to see Clarrissa. I had options. I went to bed excited, knowing I really wanted to learn how to make boats.

I was still worried about Sabattis though. There were other boat builders. Why had my father chosen an Indian? Two weeks later on a blue, still, October day we rowed to his farm on the shore of Long Lake.

It was not what I'd expected. The place looked neat and prosperous with a decent-sized frame house and a small barn. I'd been past it before but hadn't known who lived there.

Mitchell Sabattis came to greet us as my father lifted the boat out of the water. He was trim and small with a brown, weathered face. I knew he was about fifty-six and his face looked every bit that old but his body didn't. He wore a broad brimmed hat that covered his hair and shaded his face. There was a friendly look in his eye. I decided he was sober.

He spoke normal English with only a trace of an accent. I had a bag, my packbasket and my gun. He took my bag from the ground.

"He's a good boy, Mitchell, but let me know if he gives you any trouble," my father said.

"I'm sure we'll work together fine," he said.

My father picked up the bow of his boat to slide it back into the water. "I may not see you 'till the ice freezes Will. Do what Mitchell tells you." Then he was off, and I was alone with strangers.

Mrs. Sabattis was no Indian, I could tell this right away from her blue eyes and light brown hair. She was friendly and talkative, but never stopped working. She seemed to be able to do anything and talk at the same time.

I was put in a room with Harry, their youngest son, who was ten. I would start work on Monday. The next day was Sunday. As it turned out, Mitchell was a reformed alcoholic. He never drank and the Methodist Church was his pride, having himself raised much of the money to build it.

Now my concern suddenly shifted from worrying about being killed by a drunken Indian to being churched to death. My grandmother and even my father quoted scripture often, but I had rarely been expected to go to church.

As it turned out though, they never pushed it on me, but I often went for the social contact and to hear Mitchell play the violin.

Monday morning he took me into the woods, the last place I expected. "The first step in making a good boat," he said, "is finding the right wood. You ever had a good look at the ribs of your father's guide boat?"

"Sure."

"Have you noticed that the grain curves as the wood curves? You take a straight grained piece of wood and cut a curve out of it, you'll have places in the curve where the grain runs across, not down. Any spot like that is weak and breaks easy. We have to find a piece of wood that curves the same way the ribs on a boat curve."

Sure, I thought. He's trying to make a fool of me, telling me some tale like that and expecting me to believe it. I had seen crooked trees but none that crooked.

"You know your trees, don't you boy?"

"Sure."

"We're looking for spruce. Spruce knees."

"Knees?"

"Roots that have grown around something like a rock. They look like the knees of a man sitting down. You find us a good one and we'll cut it out and use it for your first guideboat."

"You mean the first one I make or the first one I get to keep?"

"Same thing. I figure if you have to row it you'll be sure to make a good one."

"The first one I make all by myself?"

"Right."

"When will that be?"

"The wood has to season and you have to pay close attention. If you learn fast and have the hand for it you could do it next winter. The winter after might be more reasonable. We'll just have to see. First you find the spruce knee."

141

Next winter, I thought. If I can do that I will have a guideboat of my own when I turn fifteen.

I looked at Mitchell. "Where's the best place around here to find spruce trees?

He smiled at me. "Good question, boy. I think you're going to learn fast."

We looked the whole day and didn't find a suitable root, but by the time we went back I knew what we were looking for.

Tuesday I watched him work. He was starting a new boat and had to cut the ribs. He hauled a spruce knee down from the loft in his shop.

"The boat tapers," he said. "I make most of my boats now tapering on both ends, like your father's. They're lighter and faster that way. Each rib is a little different in shape and size from the one next to it. I'll cut the center ribs from the outer curve."

The job took all day but he kept up a slow, quiet conversation that required me to respond and kept my attention. By the end of the day I looked at both wood and boats with more respect, and I felt I'd known my teacher all my life.

The next day he told me he needed some venison. He sent me out in his boat with my gun, an ax and a saw. He didn't have to tell me I was to keep my eyes open for both wood and deer. I came back at dusk empty handed. The next day I brought back the venison and Friday I had what I thought was a promising knee. It was heavy and I wrestled it into the boat with care, thankful that it would lose some of its weight when it had seasoned.

Mitchell praised my eye for a good curve and put it in the loft.

The next week I learned how to build the frame. Then we began working cedar strips for the siding. Each edge had to be beveled to overlap and make a smooth, watertight surface. I planed and sanded the wood until my hands blistered and the blisters gave way to callouses. The boat should weigh no more than seventy five pounds and that meant the boards must be thin.

Mitchell was not a man of surprises. He was calm and kindly and always of a consistent temperament. I asked him once why he never drank liquor.

"No good ever came of it," he said. "It was bad for me, bad for my wife and children, and I was losing money, going into debt. The Lord told me to quit, so I did. Haven't touched it since. Some people can drink it and not crave it, some can't. If I was you, boy, I'd never touch the stuff. You look too much like your father, you might have alcoholism in your blood like me."

This shocked me. I had never actually heard any-one suggest my father was an alcoholic even though I had suspected it. Even my grandmother, for all her hatred of him had never mentioned it. My father didn't even drink except in several isolated three or four day long spurts.

"You think my father is an alcoholic?" I asked.

"Oh yes."

"I think my mother died because he was drinking," I said. "Why won't he stop when he knows bad things come of it?"

"Maybe he doesn't think it's a problem. Seems to me your father doesn't even admit to himself he's an al-coholic. You've got to admit that you're doing something before you can stop."

I puzzled over that and wondered what my father would say if I brought up his drinking when he was cold sober. I had never done that; I wondered if Elizabeth had.

The Sabattis family was big and busy, and I wondered why they ever agreed to take me on. Harry was the only boy still at home, but there were six girls.

Harry liked to talk. He kept telling me his father wasn't teaching him because his parents wanted him to get more schooling. "My father will teach me though.

He taught my brothers. Isaac is one of the best boat builders around. If my father doesn't teach me Isaac will. Isaac is running for Town Clerk. He'd be a good town clerk. Some people think we shouldn't be in the government because we're Indians but Indians can do just as good a job as anyone. My father was elected Superintendent of Highways in 1866."

He went on like this every time he got the chance. Most nights I fell asleep with him still talking on his side of the bed. I could tell he was jealous because his father was teaching me. But I was jealous because he got to go to school. I wondered if I was that silly when I was ten. Then I remembered how I schemed to escape to England and was afraid of Indians and the water. I decided all ten year olds must be pretty stupid.

Harry and his sisters Dorry and Alice were in school all day and I was in the shop working. Harry was too young and talked too much to be much of a friend, Mary was too old, and Dorry was too shy.

I was busy and learning a lot. I enjoyed the work and Mitchell's company, but I wanted friends my own age. Ned was the only friend I'd made in the four years I'd lived in the mountains.

I met Hugh Jones out on the lake in early November. It was Saturday and Mitchell had sent me out to do some hunting for the family. Hugh was out for the same reason. We decided to hunt together on the other end of the lake. We raced. I was more used to paddling than rowing, so Hugh beat me by probably a quarter mile. We found several deer that day but only shot one. Since I shot it I took it.

Hugh suggested I meet with him and some other boys our age at his house Sunday morning and we'd all go hunting together. He went to school and saw them there every day. He'd get the word out.

That Sunday was cold with a wet snow falling. I didn't like hunting in this kind of weather, but I wouldn't have stayed home if I'd had a belly ache. I wanted to meet those boys.

There were five of us who set out from Jones' that day: Bob Parsons, Angus McFee, Raymond Call, Hugh and me. Raymond was fourteen and had his own boat. He took Angus with him and Bob and I rode with Hugh. Bob and Angus had older brothers and had a hard time getting rights to a boat. I didn't feel right asking to use Mitchell's on a Sunday.

We were all pretty well bundled up. I had on my trapping clothes: a new wool coat and wool pants and leather mittens. I was glad I didn't have to row. Raymond and Angus were sliding along quietly but Bob and Hugh were talking up a storm.

"Hey, Bob," Hugh was saying. "Remember last year, what we did to the stove?"

"Remember, of course I remember. That was the best one anyone ever thought up. And we never got caught."

"You're a trapper aren't you Will?"Hugh asked.

"Yeah."

"Well we took some muskrat scent my father uses for his traps and we sneaked into the school late at night when the stove was cold and smeared some on the bottom. When teacher got the stove roaring the next morning, whooee, what a smell."

I didn't even like to think of what that school must have smelled like.

"The girls all ran out screaming and holding their noses." Bob said.

"Yeah, it would have been worth getting caught just for that but we all got sent home, too," Hugh said. "And nobody ever even asked me if I'd done it, not even my father. Anybody ask you about it?"

"Sure, my father asked me," Bob said. "I just told him I didn't have any idea who done it."

"Your face was black and blue the next day." Hugh

said.

Bob looked at me. His face seemed a little red but it could have been from the cold. "Didn't have nothin' to do with that," he said quickly. "How about the time you brought in all those snakes and let them go on the floor."

They all burst out in loud laughter.

I decided hunting must have been an excuse for an outing. No deer would let us get within rifle shot with the noise we were making.

Raymond slid up beside us. "You guys keep up that noise and me and Arch will head for the other end of the lake. You better shut up. You act like a bunch of city boys."

I was embarrassed because I'd just been laughing and was suddenly aware of how loud I'd been.

"Aw, Raymond," Hugh said, "we aren't really after deer, are we? We're just out to have some fun."

"Not us," Angus said. "Raymond ain't had meat for three days and my brothers are getting on me cause I ain't shot a deer since the ice broke up last spring."

I thought Raymond looked embarrassed. "My dad's been sick," he muttered.

That shut us up. Raymond was older than the rest of us and I could tell the others looked up to him some. We slid along quietly for some time, close to shore, looking for a likely place to land. We were the front boat, and we swung around a small point of land. Hugh was rowing and I was in the stern so we didn't see the deer standing on the shore just on the other side of the point. But Bob saw it.

Maybe he'd never shot from a boat before, or he was too anxious to redeem himself after being scolded. Whatever the reason, he shot the deer kneeling in his seat with his foot braced against the gunwale. The shot sent him backwards into the water.

If Hugh had had the oars in the water at the time we would have been okay. If I hadn't been leaning a little to the starboard to see what Bob was shooting at, or even if Bob had been a little heavier and able to absorb the kick of his gun, we would have been okay. As it was, the whole boat went over.

I clung to my gun, which I had been holding in my left hand on my lap. As the boat rolled over I went backwards into the water. The shock of the cold was tremendous. I grabbed for the boat and hooked my right arm over the end. I lifted my gun up there, rested it across the boat, and looked for the others. Hugh was holding to an oar with one hand and the boat with another. Angus had Bob by the collar of his coat and Raymond was rowing him to shore.

It seemed like it took forever for them to get Bob those few feet and get him up on land. My wool clothes were heavy and my hands were already numb inside my mittens. Even my eyeballs felt frozen. Angus and Raymond towed our boat to shore with us hanging to it and we walked out of the water ourselves, our bodies shivering uncontrollably and our teeth chattering together.

We were all wearing wool and presently the water trapped in it began to heat up. This kept us from freezing to death, but we were still none too comfortable. Angus built a fire, but even that was slow in coming as most of the wood was soggy from the snow we'd been having. When the fire was big enough for all three of us to fit around it we stripped naked and held our clothes up to dry. This was slow work. Angus was kept busy breaking dead limbs off pines to feed the fire.

Raymond dressed out the deer. When he'd finished he brought over the heart. We cut it into strips and cooked it on sticks over the fire.

Now that I was warm and fed and my teeth had stopped chattering I felt sorry for Bob. Hugh was furious with him for tipping over the boat. His gun was lying in the boat and he suspected it had gone down to the bottom of the lake. Raymond and Angus were disgusted with him for doing such a fool thing as tip over the boat two, maybe three weeks before the lake froze.

Hugh got his long johns dried out first. He put them on and went with Raymond to get his boat righted. He was desperate to see if his gun was lost. It wasn't. The seat had held it in. This cheered him up but he was back to where he started with his long johns, he got so wet putting the boat to rights.

When it was just Bob and me at the fire I said, "It could have happened to any of us Bob. It was just you that saw the deer first."

I don't think he believed a word of it, but it seemed to make him feel better that at least I wasn't mad at him.

It was near dark when we got home that day. Bob tried to make peace on the way home by telling us we could all split the deer between us. After discussing it nearly all the way down the lake we decided Raymond should have the deer because he needed it the most and his hunting trip had been ruined by the accident. The rest of us had been out for a good time.

CHAPTER SIXTEEN

After our hunting trip Bob was pretty much my best friend. That's not to say that's how I wanted it to be. I appreciated his attention and gratitude, but I preferred Raymond. He was older and more sensible. Bob seemed to attract trouble. I didn't like to visit him because his father was mean and so were his older brothers. Some of the boys avoided Bob and since he was usually with me that meant they avoided me as well. This was bothersome, but I wasn't able to figure a way around it.

I was busy most of the time anyway working with Mitchell. When he took off to go hunting he gave me the option of going with him or going to school. I went to school once that winter. All the grades met in one room and were separated by rows. The teacher asked me what grade level I was on, and I told her I didn't know, the last time I was in school was five years ago in England. She told me to sit in the back and listen to all the lessons. She did them by row. The grades not being taught were expected to do their lessons or listen quietly.

"Well, William, can you tell me which grade level you fit into?" she asked.

"No, Ma'am."

"When did you find it hard to understand the lessons?"

"I didn't find any of them hard."

She gave me a suspicious look. "Are you going to be coming here regularly.?"

"No, I'm apprenticed with Mitchell Sabattis. I can only come when he's out hunting."

"Well, I guess it doesn't matter what level you're on then does it."

"I guess not, Ma'am."

After that I was no longer jealous of the others.

The lakes were frozen solid by then, and sometimes I went home for a one day visit. Once Mitchell saw my father in town and suggested I go home. I stayed with Elizabeth and Clarissa until my father came home, three days later. Elizabeth was grateful and I wished I was able to always know when he was away. I worried that she would run out of meat or hurt herself and not be able to carry water or take care of the baby.

"Don't fret, William," she said. "I try to always have enough wood chopped ahead, so I won't have to use the ax when he's gone. My chickens are still laying. I'm learning how to deal with the harsher facts of life."

Mitchell and I made eight boats that year. One of them was for Ike Kenwell, the others were for Long Lake guides. I planed and sanded and drove hundreds of the little brass tacks that held the cedar strips together.Our smallest boat weighed only fifty five pounds. I could hold it by the gunwales and lift it up over my head.

My father came to get me the first week in May. He asked Mitchell if I had learned anything.

"He'll be making himself a guideboat next year," Mitchell said.

I couldn't keep myself from grinning, though I did try.

It wasn't easy to fit back into the household. Clarissa was a year old and walking. There was an improvised gate around the steps to my loft that I had to move aside every time I went up or down. If I forgot to replace it Elizabeth became very annoyed with me because Clarissa always tried to climb the steps. Clarissa's outgrown clothes and some extra things of Elizabeth's were piled in my already crowded room.

It was good to get away from Harry's constant chatter and into my own room, but I felt like it wasn't really mine any more. It was being taken over.

Elizabeth constantly warned me not to be too loud when the baby was sleeping. It was the only time she had to get anything done.

I tried to take Clarissa out in the canoe with me,

but she kept standing up and leaning over the side. I had to keep her in front of me and tie her to my belt. It made for slow trips. I found myself wishing I had a boat to work on. "I don't really belong here anymore, do I?" I said to Elizabeth one day when she was complaining about all the laundry she had to do.

"Oh, Will, I'm sorry I've made you feel that way. It's just that this house is so small and a one year old child is so trying. She's into everything and it seems like everything poses some kind of danger. I can't even go to the outhouse and leave her here with the wash water for fear she'll drown herself.

"Well, give me a job," I said. "Just don't make me wash the diapers."

Elizabeth laughed. "You're right," she said. "I've been so busy that when you came home I just thought of you as another child to care for. You're not are you. You were doing most of this stuff for yourself years ago." She laughed again. "And two years ago when I first came you even did all the cooking. How could I have forgotten that."

So we set up the day with her doing child care in the mornings while I did the cooking and chores. After lunch I played with Clarissa and Elizabeth worked. Nap times we did Latin and French. I'd forgotten a lot.

After the flies died off we sometimes went off in the canoe visiting. The Blanchards had moved permanently to Blue the fall before but Olive Kenwell was still there. There were people with summer camps such as the Stotts on Bluff Point. Ned and his family were living at Durant's year around now. His mother and Elizabeth had visited now and then when the ice was good, so we went there often. We went to St. Hubert's Island to watch the Episcopal church being built. It was a small, high island, good for a church I supposed. Nobody would ever want to live there, it was too rocky and windswept. But the church stood out like a beacon.

Elizabeth was excited about it. To her it meant a promise of more companionship. It was finished early in the summer and we began going there every Sunday for services. People came from all over the lake in their guideboats. It was a surprise to me how many there were. Most of the women were servants and housekeepers hired by the Hotel owners and William Durant.

Hugh and Angus came once to visit me and I was pleased and flattered. I went off with them to Brown's Tract Pond to spend the night and fish.

Before my birthday my father gave me an early birthday gift. It was a little beagle puppy. I named it Britain after my old home but we called him Brit.

He gave Sammy a hard time because the dog was old and wanted to be left alone. Brit wanted to play. But Clarissa and the puppy hit it off right away. Having Brit for the baby to play with took some of the pressure off Elizabeth. I could see that I would have to take Brit off alone with me every chance I got if I wanted him to be my dog.

I turned fourteen and felt incredibly old. Next year I would have my own guide boat and do my own guiding. I would have work all summer. I figured if I worked all winter building boats and all summer guiding, by the time I turned eighteen I would have $1000.00 saved. That should be enough to pay for school. If I could get into a school.

This, as I saw it, would be my most difficult hurdle, getting into a school.Did the universities require a person to have a diploma? I was feeling quite desperate about ever reaching my goal of becoming a doctor. I was getting older but no closer, except in the matter of money.

Then one day in August a man rowed over from Long Point where he was visiting the Durants. He introduced himself as Dr. Arpad Gerster, one of my father's friends from a long time ago.My father was off with some clients at the time, so the Doctor stayed a short time and chatted with Elizabeth. He was pleasant but formal and spoke with a European accent. When he left the house I followed him. I wasn't sure how to approach him but I was afraid I wouldn't see him again so I spoke up.

"Dr. Gerster, I have a problem I need to ask you about."

He seemed a bit surprised. "Yes, what is it?"

"I want very much to be a doctor, but I'm fourteen and I haven't been to school since I was nine. How do I get into medical school. I mean how do I find out what to learn so I can get into medical school?"

He didn't scoff at me or laugh, in fact, he seemed to take me quite seriously. "There is an entrance exam. It is quite extensive. You say you haven't gone to school. Haven't your father and your stepmother been teaching you?"

"Elizabeth has taught me some French and Latin and some drawing. My father taught me to cook and hunt and swim, things like that."

He laughed. "Well, I'd say those are important things to know."

He slid his boat into the water, got into it and with much deliberation fitted the oars into the oarlocks and adjusted his hat.

He said, "The next time I come I will bring a copy of an old entrance exam. We will go over it, you and I, and we will see what you have yet to learn." He gave me a friendly nod and rowed off.

I was nearly floating with joy when I walked up the path to the house. This city doctor was going to help me. He would bring me the test and I could find out from him what books to buy to study what I needed to learn. Maybe I wouldn't be in primary school until I was twenty-four after all

Dr. Gerster hadn't said when he would be back, it

could be next week or in two years. If it was more than a few weeks how would he remember that a four-teen-year-old boy in the backwoods had high aspirations of being a doctor? I didn't think of this right away, but after a month passed and he did not come back I began to realize how faint my chances were.

By the end of August my elation and hope had deflated and I tried to make myself pretend I'd never met Dr. Gerster. The first week in September I was out working in the garden when I saw him come rowing out from behind Osprey Island. I couldn't tell for sure who it was until he was very close. But something about the shape of the hat made me run to the shore to wait.

We went out together in his boat and sat for several hours while he quizzed me. I was alternately dismayed by all the things I didn't know and surprised and elated by the many questions that were easy for me to answer. When we were finished, Dr. Gerster said, "I didn't think your father would be able to resist teaching you more than just cooking and hunting. He is a born teacher, that man."

"I don't understand," I said, "he never told me to read a single book. He never gave me lessons to study. He has always acted like he didn't really want me to be a doctor."

"But surely you didn't learn all these things about history, math and the human body when you were nine years old in school."

"Well, the books were just there in my room, with my mother's name in them and they were all I had to read for a while. And my father likes to talk so he just told me things while we were fishing or working."

He laughed "How convenient for you that your father is a doctor and not an accountant or a merchant or some other thing you don't want to be."

I suppose it was then that I began to realize that my father had been deliberately teaching me the things I needed to know, but I was still confused by the idea that it could be done with so little effort.

Dr. Gerster gave me a list of books I could read to further my education then he said, "Education is a wonderful thing, an important thing for the mind and soul of man. But it is what we learn on our own because we crave to know it that makes us what we are and stays with us all our lives."

He left me the test and the list of books and said he would look forward to seeing me next summer.

Elizabeth, Clarissa and I made a trip to Albany in October to visit her parents and with Grandfather Grayson's help I purchased a few of the books on my list.

It was harder that fall to leave home. I'd spent so much time with Clarissa that I now felt like she was really my sister. I knew she was used to having me around and thought she might miss me. I hoped she would miss me. Elizabeth would have to do all the chores and watch Clarissa too. But I had to go. I was so close to being able to make my own boat.

I was torn between leaving Brit and taking him but Elizabeth said a puppy was too much work when she already had a baby. So I took him, but I felt bad for Clarissa.

I was surprised when Mitchell set up the frame for two boats the day after I arrived. "You will start your boat now," he said. "The first one might take you all winter. It's best to go slowly as you learn. I'll be working here next to you, and you can ask me all the questions you want.

It took me three months to make it, but I often stopped for a day or two to help Mitchell.

My boat was thirteen and one-half feet long, pointed at both ends and when everything was on it it weighed sixty-one pounds. I had a hard time deciding whether to paint it the usual blue and green or a more flashy color. Red would make it stand out nicely on the water, but the blue and green blended in with the surroundings. I chose red, reasoning that no one would steal it because everyone in the woods would recognize it as mine.

My father and Elizabeth came to see it in February. It was strange to see them there because Elizabeth hadn't done much winter traveling since she'd had the baby. Clarissa rode in my father's packbasket. Her bright blue eyes peeked out over the edge and she shrieked "bubber" when she saw me.

Elizabeth was very impressed with my boat. My father walked around it many times and inspected every inch inside and out. I remembered every imperfection and hoped he didn't see them all. He was not a boat builder I reminded myself. Finally he grinned at me and said "not bad for your second winter at it. You can guide in that. Can you lift it?"

"Of course I can lift it." I had grown a lot the past year and was maybe half an inch taller than Mitchell. I could lift my boat up and over my head without getting under it first.

I made one more boat that winter and sold it to one of the summer residents who bought it for his teenage son. The money for it went to Mitchell to pay for the lumber and his teaching.

My father didn't come to pick me up that spring. I packed my bag and my packbasket and my gun into my boat. I felt so proud and free rowing along in my own boat that I had made myself. Very few people saw me. My friends were all in school. But I didn't have to depend on anyone anymore. I could go fast and carry my own boat.

At the first carry I had a bit of a setback. I had to pick up my boat with my packbasket on and carry my gun and bag at the same time. I finally tied my gun to my packbasket with a pair of socks and made a mental note to always carry some rope with me. I used a shirt to tie my bag under the stern seat. The boat was a bit of a struggle to pick up but after I adjusted its weight over my shoulders I could carry it easily enough. I went on down the carry path even more pleased with myself for having worked it all out on my own.

On the lakes I practiced my rowing and tried to get up a good steady speed. It wasn't easy with Brit jumping from one side of the boat to the other. Most of my time rowing a guideboat had been leisurely, fun time. But I would have to be serious about it now. I would be earning a living with it. I would have to get serious about training the dog too. He had to learn to sit still in the boat and to run a deer to water.

I was disappointed that no one saw me row up when I got home. My father was in the back of the house repairing some traps and Elizabeth was fixing supper. I was surprised and dismayed to see that someone was building a place very close to my father's on the north side. Did he need money that much that he would sell some of his land? I ran up the hill, very impatient to know and met my father just as he was coming out of the shed.

"Who's building on our land?" I blurted out first thing.

"I am." He laughed. "That's your workshop. You've got to have a place to build boats. It's designed just like the house. You'll have a bedroom on one side and the shop on the other."

CHAPTER SEVENTEEN

I was stunned. My own house. My own shop and bedroom. I could do everything myself, even cook. "Will I have a stove?"

My father laughed. "You've got to have a stove. How could you work without one in the winter. Your Grandfather Grayson is bringing one with him this summer. I'm not sure how we'll get it over the carries but we'll figure something out. If we wait until the ice freezes you'll miss a month or more of work time."

Until then I hadn't thought about where I was going to work. I guess I just figured I'd be with Mitchell again. But I didn't need to really, I could make boats without supervision.

My father and I worked on my house when we weren't guiding. I did more of the work than he did because I didn't get a lot of jobs. Most of what I did was trips with my father when he had groups of more than two people. I enjoyed going out with my father again and listening to his stories. And I enjoyed the people. Even the demanding and stupid ones didn't bother me like they had years before. I was a boat builder and a guide I told myself. If they knew as much as I did about this stuff they wouldn't have to hire me. I did my first guiding for pay the week before my birthday, so I could tell people I started when I was fourteen.

Just once that summer I had two patrons on my own. Mitchell got hung up with something on his farm and couldn't work that week. My father told him I was free so I went up there to meet them when they came in on the stage. I was nervous. It was one thing being out with my father and another being on my own. I thought of all the ponds I'd never been to and I hoped these men would be willing to go where I suggested.

I got there early and sat on the shore by my overturned boat. I had a book with me, but I was too preoccupied to read, so I sat whittling aimlessly on a stick. I heard the sound of oars nearby and I looked up to see a boat coming toward shore. I recognized it instantly. It was the one I had made that winter and sold.

I felt a surge of pride go from my gut up into my throat. The boy rowing it was older than I and didn't know what he was doing. He whacked his knuckles together several times then whacked the side of the boat with one of the oars. I winced and tried to see if he'd nicked the paint.

He was trying to figure out how to come to shore. Finally he took one of the oars out of its oarlock and poled himself in. He jammed the bow up onto the sand, put the oar in the boat and walked forward. As he did the boat came loose from the sand and floated backwards. He had to jump out and got his boots wet wading in with his boat in tow. As he pulled it up on the sand I said, "New boat?"

"Yes." He sounded annoyed, probably because I had seen his failed effort to come ashore dry.

I wanted to tell him I'd made his boat, but I couldn't think of a smooth way to do it. "Been to any of the other lakes with it yet?" I asked, knowing he hadn't from the way he handled the boat. He probably hadn't figured out how to pick it up yet. I desperately wanted to give him a lesson. At the rate he was going the creation I had worked on for months would be destroyed by the end of the summer.

"No, we've been too busy building our cottage, that new one over there." He pointed nonchalantly across the lake. He was trying to impress me. It was a big building for just one family. I'd seen it going up all summer. It looked nearly finished.

I started to tell him my name, but he went on, "I haven't seen you around, are you one of the local farmer boys?"

"No, I live on Raquette Lake. I'm a guide and I'm

here to pick up some of my patrons."

He snorted. "Right, and I'm the Queen of England. Kid, I think you're going to be in trouble if your daddy finds out you've been telling whoppers along with skipping out of chores." He laughed and walked on up to the store.

I wanted to say something back, but couldn't think what. Instead, I pulled his boat farther up the beach so it wouldn't float away and inspected it to see how much damage he'd done to it since he'd had it. Considerable scrapes in the paint and a gouge out of one of the ribs. I heartily wished someone else owned it, someone who knew the value of a boat.

The stage came and I walked up to the hotel to meet my patrons. I heard someone say, "Mitchell Sabattis?"I hurried to meet the two men I would be guiding. "Hello," I said. "Mitchell can't make it. He asked me if I would fill in for him. My name is Will Chadwick." The boy with my guideboat was standing nearby with an angry look. "Is your daddy's name Will Chadwick, too?" he asked as I walked past.

"No," I said. "I'm the only Will Chadwick in this part of the country."

Now he knew, I thought. Now he knew that I was not only really a guide but that I built his boat. I could tell he hated me for it but right then I only cared that he knew.

My two patrons were very polite, but I could tell they were disappointed to have a substitute guide that was so young. "Do you have a destination in mind?" I asked them.

"No, we're fishermen, after bass mostly."

I was tremendously relieved but tried not to show it."I can take you to a lot of good spots for bass. Do you want to fish in one spot or do you want to see the lakes?"

"We'd like to move around, a different spot each day if we could."

It was easier than I could have imagined. They were serious fishermen. I cooked and rowed and even told a story now and then. I told some of my father's and some of my own. It went well. It helped that they'd never been on the lakes, never met Mitchell and had no one to compare me with. They caught fish and at the end of the week they even asked me to guide for them again next year. My first regular patrons. I felt triumphant.

I went home and worked on my shop with new confidence.

Clarissa hung around me much of the time and asked hundreds of questions about nothing important, questions like: "What color is that? What is this spot? What are you looking at?" It made my work go slowly, but most of the time I was glad to have her company. Sometimes I kept her with me while Elizabeth went out in the canoe.

When Grandmother and Grandfather Grayson came that year they brought my stove with them. They spent the first night at the Prospect House in Blue, for the novelty of it. This was the first Hotel in the world to have electric lights in all the rooms. It even had a two story outhouse connected to the hotel so the people on the top floor wouldn't have to go downstairs in the night, and a steam elevator for those who didn't want to bother climbing stairs.

The hotel was new so we all went to meet the Grayson's to have a look at it. No one else on the lakes had electric lights. They were run by a generator which was in a house of its own. My favorite thing was the elevator, and I found as many excuses as I could to ride it. The place had 300 rooms and could sleep 500 people. We all thought it was very grand and modern except my father who said it was a monstrosity and ruined the looks of the lake.

Plenty of people were flocking to it, though. When

we rowed in, the porch was busy with people chatting in groups. At one end there was a young man playing a banjo. Several young women were gathered around him singing and laughing. I felt a pang of envy and wished I could be a part of it.

My stove had been left on the ground in its wooden crate. My father pried the crate open to see if the stove could be taken apart. We didn't need the extra bulk of the crate anyway. There was at least half an hour of discussion between us about how to load it and how to distribute the weight between the two boats. Grandmother Grayson grumbled that she didn't see why the stove had to come on the stage with them. They could have shipped it later.

"But then I wouldn't have been here to help, my dear," Grandfather Grayson said.

"Perhaps mother and Clarissa and I could spend the night here to make more room in the boats," Elizabeth said.

I wanted to offer to stay, too, but it was my stove.

When we left I was carrying Elizabeth, Clarissa, Grandmother Grayson and all the luggage in my boat. My father had the stove in the bow of his and Grandfather Grayson in the stern. The wood from the crate was arranged along the bottom and up the inside of the boat to keep the stove from bashing against the ribs or the siding.

This arrangement was fine. It was the Marion River Carry that was the problem. We made two trips, the first with the boats and luggage. The women stayed with the boats while we went back for the stove. Grandfather Grayson and I had a friendly argument about which of us would carry the wood and which would help my father with the stove. We agreed that we would take turns.

It was an awkward thing to carry, not horribly heavy, because it was only a small wood stove. But the one holding the top had nothing to grab onto. We were just out of sight of Utowana Lake when my father said "Stop, this is stupid." We set the thing down and he made a platform out of the wood from the crate. We carried it the rest of the way with comparative ease.

I enjoyed the Grayson's visit very much that year. I had my half finished house to stay in and my own work to do. When they went back to Albany I went with them. I had to buy my own tools and the tacks and screws for putting my boats together.

By the end of September my house was finished. I built myself a bed and a workbench, then got my shop set up. I even had a work order. Frederick Durant wanted boats to rent at the Prospect House-- some guideboats, some canoes, he would take whatever I made that year. I picked up my seasoned spruce knees from Mitchell and set out finding more for next year's work. I never went hunting without my saw. I missed several deer that should have been easy meat, but I stocked my attic with cedar and spruce.

That winter I made four boats and a sledge. The latter was for the family. It had runners and two handles in back, so the one using it could push it along the snow. It was for hauling supplies in winter. I designed it so that it would float high and dry with two people and some supplies. It looked a little like a strange boat on runners but it worked. I even made a little paddle to carry in it. My father and I tried it out on the ice just before spring breakup. It worked great from the ice to the shore but we couldn't pull it from the water up onto the rotten ice.

"That's okay," my father said. "It floats great. We aren't going to deliberately go out on bad ice anyway."

But my other experiment that winter turned out just the way I wanted. I built a very small guide boat, designed for a woman or a boy. It was 10 1/2 feet long and weighed forty five pounds. Elizabeth could lift it and carry it up the hill from the lake. It would carry her and Clarissa easily if she stayed out of the rougher water. I gave it to her and she was very pleased. She said she didn't know when she'd have the time to go gallivanting in the summer but it was wonderful to be able to if she wanted. I knew how she felt.

That was a good winter for me. I had my own shop and was back with my family. I could help out when my father was gone. I ran the trap line a few times when he was off on a drunk, but other than that no trapping. I could be with the family if I wanted or alone. I was working, but I still had time to study. I could not give up my desire to be a doctor. It was part of me, part of how I saw myself.

I saw more of Ned that winter than I had in two years. For once I was busier than he was. He came over often to watch me work and ask questions about it. He helped me quite a bit with the sanding and tacking. He loved doing anything with wood.

"The way I see it," Ned said, "if I'm going to stay here on the lakes it wouldn't hurt to learn how to build boats. I'm primarily a carpenter, of course, always will be. But it wouldn't hurt to be able to build boats."

I could tell doing wood work in my own shop raised me up some in Ned's esteem.

"You're always welcome," I said. "Besides, if I hadn't tagged around after you I wouldn't have known enough to be able to finish this shop."

CHAPTER EIGHTEEN

That summer I had plenty of work. More and more people were coming to the lakes. Frederick Durant liked the work I did on the boats and he recommended me to his patrons. This meant that I was often at Blue. That pleased me because there was a girl there working as a maid at the Prospect House who was about my age. I liked the way she looked and connived to run into her whenever possible. Her name was Jenny, and I even had the chance to talk to her for about half an hour one day when she was eating her lunch, and I was waiting for a patron.

She didn't say much. I decided she was shy and probably a bit in awe of me because I was one of the guides. But I did discover that she planned on working there next summer and she was studying to be a teacher. I decided the next time I had a day with no work I'd come by and see if she had some free time to go out in the boat with me.

Five days later I woke up at dawn, ate a quick breakfast of bacon and biscuits and was off. I wanted to get there early enough so I would have the best chance possible of catching her when she was free. I wasn't sure how I would find out her schedule. The Prospect House was a big place and I couldn't run from room to room looking for her. I guessed I would probably have to ask someone in the kitchen if they knew where she was.

I was mulling this over in my mind, getting more and more nervous and more full of anticipation when I rounded the first bend in the Marion and nearly ran smack into another boat. It was crosswise the river and the fellow in it was just sitting. He looked startled when he saw me. I veered off toward the bushes at the edge of the water and managed to miss hitting him. He looked like he'd had a bad night's sleep and he hadn't shaved in maybe 2 days. I didn't recognize him. I recognized the boat. It had a new coat of paint but it was one of mine, the one I'd made right after the one I was rowing.

I looked again at the man in it. It was him all right, the rich guy from Long Lake. Someone must have taught him how to use the boat. He'd managed to get it over two carries and the paint job was pretty much intact. What was he doing there at that hour of the morning?

The last time I'd seen him he was giving me a look of hate. This time he was smiling, but it was a flustered, surprised sort of smile. I got the impression he'd been expecting me but just not so soon. I thought this was unlikely and as I had other things on my mind I grabbed my paddle and tried to maneuver around him. The river there was wide enough for both of us end to end but he wasn't letting me get by him easily.

"Aren't you Will Chadwick?" he asked.

"Of course." I couldn't believe he had forgotten that little exchange at long Lake last summer.

"I'm Tom Jackson from up on Long Lake."

"Sure, I remember you, you've got one of my boats." I really didn't want to talk. I wanted to be on my way.

"You on your way to pick up a sportsman?"

"No, just out to pay a call on someone."

"I'll come along then if you don't mind. It's my first time this far south. I don't really know my way around."

I realized I'd made a mistake. I shouldn't have told him that. "You don't really need a guide if you're going to Blue," I said. "Just follow the river until you can't pass through with your boat. There's a path there. Follow it to the next lake then it's straight going the whole way. Utowana and Eagle Lakes are long and narrow. You can't get lost on them."

I rowed on but I wasn't going to lose him on the river, the turns were too constant for me to get up any speed. He dogged me. Bob Parsons has been telling me all about you," he said. "Bob seems to think you'd be a good one to teach me about the lakes and guiding. Maybe get me started on it."

It must have been obvious I was trying to get away from him but he never let up. Finally I gave up and let him come up next to me. I realized I would have to change my plans for the day. I didn't want him following me into the Hotel and listening to me blunder my way through a meeting with Jenny.

"Where did you sleep last night?" I asked.

"On the top of that rocky bluff just at the entrance to the river."

No wonder he looked so awful.

"Okay", I said, "If you want to be a guide this is your first lesson; don't camp near a swampy area. This whole river runs through a swamp. Set up camp where the ground is high and the trees are a good size and try to pick a spot where you might get a bit of a breeze."

A look passed over his face like it had the first time I met him, a proud and angry look. But it went as fast as it came, like a shadow. I could almost wonder if I had been mistaken. Maybe he thought I was laughing at him. Well, I was laughing at him.

"The mosquitoes were a bit thick last night," he said. "I thought that was normal."

"Oh, they're always around, it's just some places are worse than others." I decided he hadn't spent many nights outside that palace he lived in. I started feeling guilty for the way I was treating him. Maybe he just wanted to make friends.

"Look," I said, "This is really an easy trip, from here to Blue. Since I have the day off why don't I take you up Brown's Tract to Eighth Lake. It's a long carry but I'm not in any hurry. Are you?

"No, what's at Eighth Lake, any town?"

"Oh no, it's all pretty wild. There's a whole chain of Lakes. You can go all the way to Old Forge. It takes maybe a day."

"Can we do that today?"

I didn't want to go to Old Forge. I had another day free and I wanted another go at seeing Jenny. Also, I didn't come prepared to spend the night, no fishing gear, no food. I didn't even have my gun.

"I don't think we'd better unless you brought some food or some fishing gear."

"I thought guides could live off the land. You mean we couldn't find enough to eat to see us through till to-morrow."

"I suppose we could if you don't mind living on cattail root and blueberries."

"I'd like to try it. I've never done anything like that before. I'm eighteen and it's the first time my father has let me stay out overnight."

"Really," I said. "I've been going out on my own since I was eleven." I started to feel sorry for the guy. He needed a real adventure. He needed to see what it was like to have to work for your food.

"How old are you now?"

"Sixteen." It sounded so young next to eighteen. He was probably going to a University that fall, being a rich man's son. "I guess we'd better only go to Inlet if you've never been out on your own before. It would be pushing it to try to get to Old Forge."

"I want to go all the way to the next town," he said.

"Inlet is the next town, Old Forge is just the last town on the chain of Lakes."

"Okay, let's do it."

I led the way back down river. I pointed out a bird to him now and then and told him the names. He said he wasn't much interested in birds. I told him he had to learn the names of things if he wanted to be a guide. People would ask him and expect him to know.

He laughed. "I guess you're right. I'll try to pay

more attention."

We hit the lake and all conversation ended. The water was still morning calm and there was so much open lake ahead I knew I wouldn't lose him. I rowed hard and left him behind. I couldn't help but show off a bit. I kept going until I reached Big Island. He hadn't rounded Long Point yet so I waited for fear I'd lose him. When he came in sight I struck off again and waited for him off Brown's Tract Inlet.

When Tom caught up he was breathing very hard and sweat was running down his forehead though the morning was still cool. I felt bad. Maybe I'd overdone it.

I tried to pretend I didn't notice how winded he was. I just said, "This is it. We'll have to use our paddles the rest of the way to the carry. It'll be slow going for the next two miles."

We paddled along quietly for maybe a quarter of an hour then Tom said, "Well, Chadwick, you're a boat builder and a guide. You've got your future set and you've learned your trade already. I hope you know how lucky you are with your simple life. I have to go to university and wear my brain out studying all year. My parents expect me to become a lawyer."

"Is that why you want to become a guide?" I asked. "Do you want to escape to a simpler life? Have you been reading Thoreau?"

"Sure, I think you've got the life. And you don't have to worry about grades or keeping up with your class."

"Oh, I will soon enough. In a couple of years I'll take the entrance exams for medical school then I suppose I'll get caught up in all that."

I heard a strange sound behind me like he was choking. But when I turned around he looked composed and was smiling.

"Medical school, huh. Now why would you want to go and do a thing like that?"

"Actually, my grandparents had planned for me to go to law school but when they died and I moved here I decided I was much more interested in being a doctor." Something kept me from telling him about my father. If he didn't already know, I didn't want to be the one to tell him. "But I'm looking forward to school. I haven't gone since I was nine. I used to enjoy it."

"If you haven't been to school all this time how do you expect to get into medical school." I couldn't see his face but he sounded like it had a sneer on it.

"Oh I have all the reading material I need and I have copies of old entrance exams. I study in the winter when I'm not working on my boats. I study when my patrons are fishing. I really get quite a lot of reading done. Do you really not want to be a lawyer?"

"I never said I didn't want to be a lawyer," he snapped. I just don't like the University. It's dull."

I felt I must have said the wrong thing so I shut up for a while. Then we came to the carry.

The carry there from Brown's Tract Inlet into Eighth Lake is long, over a mile, and I began to wonder if he was up to it. He was tall, at least four inches taller than me, and he wasn't overweight, but the row across Raquette made me question his endurance. I would have to try not to go too fast and I'd stop for a rest if he started to act tired. We pulled up our boats.

"Why don't you go first?" I said.

That was the longest, most tortuous carry I've ever done. He was such a slow walker. I would never have thought a tall person could walk that slowly. I took to stopping until he was out of sight then catching up to him and stopping again. When he realized what I was doing he protested and said I was resting and making him keep on going. He thought I was trying to wear him out and declared that he was going to take rests too. After that we rested more than we walked. I tried to get around him so I could go my own pace but he blocked my way and said I was trying to get ahead and find some food without him.

The way he was acting he couldn't have been too concerned with making friends. Or maybe he was always this way and didn't have any friends. Maybe that was why he didn't like his school.

I decided he was really hungry. Maybe he hadn't had breakfast. Could be he hadn't eaten since he left Long Lake. A person like that, used to being taken care of, might not even think of food until he needed it.

"Are you hungry?" I asked.

"Of course I'm hungry."

"You should have said something sooner. We passed a good patch of blueberries about fifteen minutes ago."

The way we were traveling, fifteen minutes ago wasn't very far. We decided to leave our boats and go back.

"Okay, here we are," I said and started to eat. I was hungry enough myself.

"You're eating them all yourself."

"I am not, there are plenty. It would take us all day to pick all the berries here."

"But you aren't picking any for me. What kind of guide are you? I thought a good guide was supposed to provide the food. All you found for me are berries and you're eating them all yourself."

"In the first place a guide doesn't provide food. He shows his patrons how to get it themselves. I don't fish or hunt for the sportsmen, they do that. Why should I pick your berries? In the second place, you aren't even paying me. I'm not your guide. If you want to eat you'd better do it or we'll never even get as far as Inlet."

He had no answer to that. He started to eat, picking the berries, one at a time and popping them into his mouth. Fortunately I was prepared. When I had eaten my fill I took my book out of my leather satchel I always carried with my matches and knife in it. It was a book on anatomy. I settled down with it, my back against a tree.

Tom finally finished eating and came over to where I was reading. He looked at my book and the mean look crossed his face again.

"Don't you think we aught to get up and get moving if we expect to reach that town tonight," he said.

"We don't have to go to Inlet. We can camp wherever we are when it gets dark then head back in the morning."

"I want to get to the town. For one thing, I'm going to need a decent meal," he said.

For one thing, I thought, what's the other thing? I really wondered why it was so important for him to get to a town. I thought of my first trip into the mountains. I wanted to get to a town so I could escape from my father and go back to the city. Maybe that's what he wanted. But he was a grown man, why couldn't he just do that in Long Lake. Why drag me into it. By now I realized that talk about living the simple life and maybe becoming a guide was just so much babble.

We made our slow way to Eighth Lake and I was heartily relieved to be in my boat again. I took it easy on the lake. I was in no great hurry to get to the next carry.

It was late enough when we got to Fourth Lake that we couldn't have gone any farther if we wanted to. We'd passed a little inn on the carry and I wanted to make camp and wait for him while he went there to eat. I had no money with me to buy a meal. He was suddenly very expansive and wanted to buy dinner for me. I didn't argue. He'd been enough trouble to me that day. I felt I certainly had earned a meal and I was hungry. But I insisted we find a spot to sleep first. I never like doing that in the dark.

We left our boats at our camping spot and walked back along the path to the inn. There were five men in there eating or sitting at the bar. Two of them I recognized, but I didn't know them well. The others were probably their patrons. I'd been through here enough times to know the owner, but I wasn't chummy with him like my father was.

We had a good meal of steak and potatoes with blueberry pie for dessert. I was finishing up when Tom said "let me buy you a drink."

"No thanks," I said.

"No thanks? I am offering to buy you a drink. You don't say no when someone offers to buy you a drink. That's not polite. Have you lived in the backwoods so long you don't even know common courtesy? That's it! I'll give you a second chance now that you know. I'll buy you a drink."

I'd never had a drink. I'd smelled my father's medicinal whiskey and that was enough to discourage me. But my father's drinking sprees had me worried too. Mitchell said I looked a lot like my father, maybe I would be an alcoholic too. Mitchell had warned me to stay away from the stuff.

"I really don't want a drink."

Tom laughed. "You've never had a drink before, have you?" He was being very loud. The whole room could hear him and some of the men were looking over at us and grinning. "Here you are strutting around the woods, calling yourself a guide and you're just a kid, wet behind the ears." He turned to the men at the bar. "He calls himself a guide. He brings me out here, no food, no fishing gear, no gun and now he tells me he's never had a drink." He turned back to me. "Boy, all men drink. I've seen your father in the bar telling stories. He can really hold his liquor. What happened to you?"

One of the men yelled, "Hey ain't you Ben Chadwick's boy? How come you never learned to drink. Whiskey should have been mother's milk to you."

That bit about no fishing gear, gun or food was

175

embarrassing, and I wasn't in any position to do explaining without sounding foolish. I had six men watching me and waiting for my decision. I knew another "no" would just make them keep it up. A "yes" would shut them up. I thought about it.

My grandfather and his friends had drunk plenty of alcohol but I had never seen one of them drunk. Elizabeth had said to me that all men drink. Mitchell didn't drink, but he was religious. Religious people were different but even some of them drank. I'd seen them in church on Sunday and going into the bar week nights. Maybe I was making a big deal out of nothing. I hated my father's drinking when I was a child and had to be alone. So what? Nothing had happened. Maybe all men really did drink. I decided it was easier to take the whiskey Tom offered me than try to fight a nonsensical battle.

The stuff tasted bad, but it had a certain after effect that seemed to compensate. The men watched me take that first drink like I was going through some ancient ritual. I tried not to make a face. When it was down the men in the room became very jolly and Tom especially was cheerful, happier than I'd seen him.

I woke up the next day underneath a pine tree next to the carry trail. Brit was lying with his head on my leg. I felt terrible. I was convinced someone had bashed me over the head with something. But why would they do that. My boat. Someone must have wanted to steal my boat. There was nothing else they could have wanted. My leather bag was still slung around my neck with everything in it. I jumped up and started to run for the lake to check on my boat. I'd have a lot of walking and maybe some swimming to do if I lost it.

Just around the first bend in the trail I came in sight of the Inn. In my confusion I had run in the wrong direction. Feeling like a fool I turned back. I was walking now and I felt my head. No bumps or bruises. Something was making it hurt and I was feeling sick.

Perhaps the meat in my dinner was spoiled.

I reached the lake and found my boat where I'd left it. Tom was not there and his boat was gone. I wondered briefly if I should wait for him then decided he must have gone back without me. I would catch up to him soon enough if he had. If he hadn't, well I was sick of him anyway.

I drank a good deal of water and waited for my stomach to calm down a bit, which it did, but I could have used some biscuits. I was hungry again, too hungry considering the huge meal I'd eaten the night before.

My head still ached, but I lifted my boat up over my head and started back along the trail. I had patrons to pick up in Long Lake the next day.

I caught up to Tom on Seventh Lake, caught up to him and passed him.

"Some guide you are," he hollered at me as soon as I was within earshot. "You can't hold your liquor and you threw up all over me while I tried to get you back to camp. You passed out and left me to make my way home by myself. If you're the same kind of boat builder as you are a guide I hope I make it back before my boat falls apart. Little Willie Chadwick, think you can do what a man can do and you can't even hold a shot of liquor down." He laughed and may have said more, but I was well past him by then.

I didn't know whether I had had one shot or ten. I could only remember back to the first. But he must have been right about losing my dinner. That would explain my ravenous hunger.

I rowed as fast as I could, and at the carries I nearly ran until I was so hungry I was forced to slow down. I stopped to eat berries, but I was loath to stay long at it. I knew Tom could never catch up to me yet I felt pursued, and I didn't want to ever see him again.

I thought over it all as I walked. He never really

acted as though he liked me and he often looked like he hated me. Why would he want to go on a trip with me? For that matter, what was he doing drifting across Marion River at that hour of the morning? Was he waiting for me, looking for me? He wanted to get to a town so badly. Was he just looking for a chance to make a fool of me in front of some other guides? Would anyone go to that much trouble to do that? Why? Was I just making it all up in my head? Why me anyway? Maybe he was only out looking for diversion, and I happened to come by. Whatever the case, I didn't like him.

I had a hard time getting him off my mind, he had made such a fool of me.

I tried thinking about Jenny and the next time I would have a chance to see her. I had a job tomorrow that would last six days then I had another job out of Blue that would take me four days. Then I had three days until my next patrons out of Blue again. Maybe I could get to see Jenny when I went to pick up my patrons next week. I could ask her in advance if she had some time to go out in the boat with me. Maybe I could even take her up the mountain and show her the lakes. Maybe if she knew in advance she could arrange some time off.

I was having some luck forgetting about Tom by thinking about Jenny. I thought up whole conversations with her, things I would ask her. I even imagined I might kiss her.

CHAPTER NINETEEN

I spent that night at home and rose early the next morning so as to be in Long Lake to meet my patrons. I would be guiding the two bass fishermen from last year.

I wondered where Tom was. I didn't want to have to talk to him, but even more than that I didn't want to get stuck behind him on a carry. I supposed he was at one of the hotels sleeping late. I thought again about our early morning meeting two days before. It had to have been planned. He didn't seem the type to get up early if he hadn't a reason. Besides, he was just sitting there on the river.

It suddenly occurred to me that my bright red boat gave anyone who was looking for me a definite advantage. From a distance most of the guide boats looked alike with their blue and green paint.Mine was the only red one around and was easily spotted, even from a mile or more away. I began to give serious thought to repainting it.

I wondered why Tom had worked so hard just to get me drunk.

I met Morton and Edgar, the fishermen, at about noon and we lost no time getting out on the lake. They traveled light, with the bulk of their gear the food staples they brought. I took them north because I had taken them south the year before and because I wanted to avoid running into Tom on his way back home.

My time with these two men was pleasant and uneventful except for one incident. Our second day out we rounded a point and came upon some sportsmen and their guides waiting offshore for the dogs to drive the deer to water. We could hear the dogs yipping in the distance. Brit cocked his ears forward and put his paws on my seat to look out.

"Will, do you mind if we pass over to the other side of the lake?" Morton said. His voice sounded a bit tense, so without answering I turned the boat and rowed for the other side.

"Thank you," he said. "I didn't want to be present when the deer came out of the woods. The way the hunting is done here does not seem like sport to me. Force the deer to water, row up beside it, grab the poor beast by the tail then shoot it. I don't see how that is any more sport than shooting cattle in their pens. And then they come back to their hotels bragging about the chase. I don't like to watch it."

I hadn't thought of it before, but after Morton's outburst I couldn't help but think of it every time I set out to run the deer. Though I still enjoyed a night hunt, the day hunt was spoiled for me. The way he put it made it seem worse than trapping.

When that week was over I dropped Morton and Edgar off at the hotel and rowed over to Hugh's. His mother greeted me the way she always did; with food. "Hugh is out fixing some fence. He'll be back soon. You just sit down and have some lunch. You've been eating nothing but your own cooking for weeks if I know you."

"But Mrs. Jones, I'm a good cook. What is this, chicken?"

"Of course it's chicken. If we didn't eat at least two of those birds a week we'd be overrun with them."

"Well, all I've had for a week is fish. Nothing could smell or look so good as this." I ate heartily. No matter how much you like your own cooking it is always nice to eat someone else's now and then.

Hugh came in as I was finishing. "Will, great!" he said. "Have you got an extra day? A bunch of us are going across the lake on a campout. Want to come?"

"Leave it to a bunch of farmers to get excited about a campout."

Hugh was the only one I could say something like that to. He liked being a farmer.

"All right, I can see that might not be the most fun

thing for you to do," he said. "But you haven't done any-thing with us all year."

"Who's coming?"

"Bob, Angus, and a couple of summer guys."

"Tom Jackson?"

"Of course not," Hugh said. "I wouldn't ask you to come if he was going to be there. He's been telling stories about you."

"He didn't waste any time, did he. You know, Hugh, I can't figure out why he went to all that trouble to make me look like a fool."

"He hates you."

"How could he hate me, before last week he didn't even know me."

"Well, he knew you made his boat and he knew you were a guide. It's pretty obvious you're younger than he is."

"So?" I pretended I didn't understand, but I understood well enough. I'd been having a pretty good time gloating over those things. But Tom couldn't have known one way or the other if I even thought about it. "For all he knows I'm jealous of his money and his chance to go to the University."

"I think it's Bob," Hugh said. "I don't think he misses the chance to talk you up."

"Bob?" Now I was really confused. "What does Bob have to do with Tom Jackson? They don't seem like a very likely pair."

"They stick pretty close. The way I see it Bob is really impressed with Tom's money and just the fact that Tom is older and pays attention to him. Tom loves to have a hanger on, someone he can impress, someone who will always agree with him. The only problem is Bob still thinks you are the most important fellow around. He hasn't figured out that Tom doesn't agree with him."

I hadn't seen Bob much the past year. Hugh was

my favorite and his family always welcomed me, so I dropped in on him as often as I could. But Bob's family was surly. I didn't like to go there, and there didn't ever seem like much to talk about with Bob.

"So if Bob and Tom are such good friends why isn't Tom going camping with you tonight?"

"Oh, he hangs around with one person at a time. Tom's not the sort who would be comfortable with the whole gang of us."

"All right, I guess I'd better go on this trip. You've got me curious to see how Bob is doing."

"He's been drinking a lot. His father found out and kicked him out of the house. He sleeps in the barn and his mother sneaks him food when she can. But it isn't easy getting things by the old man and the brothers."

"What does he eat then?"

"He hunts and fishes. All of us guys bring him stuff and have him over now and then. Maybe Tom helps him. I don't know."

"What will he do when winter comes?"

"Don't know, maybe his father will cool off by then."

Our conversation was interrupted by Angus who came over with one of the summer guys. The newcomer's name was Don. They both carried full pack baskets.

I teased them a little about all the stuff they carried for just one night. I had to do it. I was the professional camper. It was a mistake. Angus had been waiting for an opening like that. I could see it in his face.

"I don't know Will, what I've been hearing about you, you might be better off if you carried a little more on your overnight trips."

He was grinning and I knew he was just waiting to see what I'd say.

"What have you been hearing about me, Angus," I said, and I tried to grin back.

"Heard you'd have starved to death if it hadn't been for Tom Jackson."

"That's interesting," I said. "I didn't know it was possible to starve to death in one day. Probably would have starved to death though if I'd been stuck behind him on any more carries."

Hugh laughed. "Good answer, Will."

Angus didn't say anything else then, but I knew from past experience and the look on his face that he wasn't going to let anything get by. I'd eventually have to answer questions about the whole embarrassing mess. And who knew what Tom had made up.

We all went to the lake and loaded their stuff in the boats. Angus rode with Hugh and I took Dan. He wasn't much of a talker but I could tell he was at ease in the boat and content to be where he was.

We rowed along the shore toward the cabin of the other summer kid whose name was Albert. About halfway there Bob waved at us from a large, flat rock. I was closest to shore, so I pulled in and picked him up.

As usual, I couldn't think of much to say to Bob. I didn't want to let on Hugh had told me about his troubles. "How did school go this year?" I asked him. I figured it was a safe one. From what I knew he liked school and did fairly well.

"I didn't go this year. My father said I was too old for it, he needed me on the farm. But Tom Jackson says he thinks he can get me into his school even though I did quit early. You haven't been going to school at all and you're planning on going to a university aren't you Will?"

Bob always amazed me. He came from such a mean and poor family; they treated him very badly, but he was never mean himself. He seemed almost like a buffoon, blundering around and so often getting things wrong. Yet he usually acted like the best was coming to him, maybe tomorrow, maybe next week. When I wasn't around him I didn't think of him much but when I was with him I always felt terribly sorry for him.

"Sure," I said. "I've been studying to pass an entrance exam. You're smart, Bob, you ought to be able to do that."

"That's what Tom says."

I didn't want to ask him where he was going to get the money. Everything about his life seemed so hopeless to me, and he was so hopeful, I hated to ruin it for him.

We picked up Albert and between him and Angus the rest of us didn't have to worry about making conversation.

We headed for a lean-to up the lake on the other side. It was an easy spot to land and pull up the boats and it usually caught a breeze, if there was one.

Everybody but Bob had brought some food, but except for a small piece of bacon I had there wasn't any meat. After we unloaded into the lean-to we all went back out to fish.

We'd been sitting with our lines in the water maybe ten minutes when Albert said, "I hate fishing." He said it rather loudly and it startled me a bit because everyone had been quiet.

"Is it true that the fish won't bite if they hear you talking?" Angus asked.

"That's what I've heard," Hugh said. "What do you think Will?"

"A lot of the fishermen say that and I humor them," I said. "But my father and I always talk when we fish. I've never noticed that we have worse luck than anyone else."

"That settles it then," Angus said. "Let's talk."

"What's there to talk about?" Albert said. "It seems like all anyone does around here is fish, hunt and farm. I don't see how my father can stand it. I don't see how all of you fellows stand it."

"What would you be talking to your friends back

home about?" Hugh asked.

"Girls, school, what kinds of jobs we'll have in four or five years."

Angus laughed. "Sounds pretty much like what we talk about here. Come on Albert, ain't you got no originality? If you're going to gripe at least you could make up something interesting."

"Really now. I suppose you're all planning on going off to Europe this fall. And you, Angus, are planning on becoming a famous grammarian, I can tell.

"You trying to tell me you don't like my double negatives?" Angus said.

I was surprised Angus didn't take a poke at him right there in Hugh's boat. Normally he had a quick temper and spoke more with his fists than his mouth. I was ready to belt the guy myself.

"If you don't like the company what are you doing here?" Dan said. "You seem more like Tom Jackson's type. Why don't you hang out with him?"

I looked at Bob to see if he was going to say anything, but he was baiting his hook and had his head down so I couldn't see his face. I wondered if he knew how much everyone else didn't like Tom. I wondered if he had heard the stories Tom was telling around about me.

"Oh, I don't mean anything insulting," Albert said. "I'm just sick of wasting time in the woods, listening to my father talk about fishing. I'm so sick of hearing about fishing and eating fish and fighting off the bugs. I want to get on with my life."

Albert kept his mouth shut the rest of the time we spent fishing. He didn't catch anything. Bob caught a perch and a small trout. Hugh and I each caught a bullhead and Dan brought up a good-sized whitefish. That was enough for a meal, so we rowed on back to the lean-to. The sun was setting by the time we got back, so I got started on the dinner while Hugh made a fire and

Dan and Bob cleaned the fish.

It was a good meal. I fried up the last of my bacon and split the fat between two pans. In one pan I fried potatoes and pushed them all to one side while I cooked the fish. In the other pan I made cornbread. Hugh had brought a mess of greens from his mother's garden. I cooked them in a pot with salted water. Angus had a pail of blueberries and we ate them for dessert.

When the meal was over Angus pulled a bottle of whiskey out of his pack basket. Albert said he'd brought a bottle, too, and produced a large one of rum.

I groaned inside. A drinking party. If I knew Angus, he would probably try to get me drunk, so he could see if Tom Jackson had been telling the truth. I was going to have to go through the whole thing over again, having to decide whether to drink with them or not. If I didn't I'd have to put up with at least as much ridicule as I had from Tom. I knew Angus well enough. He'd glory in seeing me make a fool out of myself. Then the thought hit me that if I did drink I'd make even more a fool of myself. Passing out and losing my dinner would be things I'd never hear the end of and Angus was just dying to get that chance. Maybe some of the others were too.

I looked at Bob. He had a worried expression on his face. I wondered why. He'd surely heard Tom's stories. Maybe he thought I was going to take Angus' bait.

"All right, my fine fellows. Here's where the fun begins. We've got two bottles here. Hey, Bob, you must have brought some. Two bottles ain't enough for six of us."

Bob looked sullen, which surprised me. I'd never seen him look anything but cheerful or contrite.

"Come on, Bob, you trying to hoard them all for yourself."

Slowly Bob turned to his pack basket and pulled out a bottle of whiskey.

"That's better," Angus said. "Now we're up to one half bottle a piece."

I took a deep breath. "You've got more than that, I said. "I'm not drinking." I figured I'd have the advantage if I made the first move.

They all looked a little surprised. Hugh was behind me. I couldn't see him.

"Why not?" Angus said. He had a sly grin on his face.

"You guys all heard Tom's story. I can't hold liquor. Why should I make myself a laughingstock more than once." That must have been the right thing to say. They all looked at each other; no one said anything.

"I'm not drinking anything either," Hugh said. "I think I'll have more fun watching."

So Hugh and I watched them drink, but I can't say we had fun. For the first bit I was watching Bob. He wasn't drinking but he kept his gaze on a bottle constantly and he looked desperately thirsty. Finally he gave in. With an angry look on his face he grabbed a bottle and drank several gulps in a row. I remembered the taste of the stuff I'd had at the Inn and wondered how anyone could gulp it.

After that Bob took part in the conversation and seemed to be happy. The others were getting drunk.

Angus and Albert were not getting along very well. Dan left and went around behind the lean-to. That left no obstruction between them and within seconds they were slugging at each other. They never stood up. It seemed very strange watching two people having a fist fight sitting down. Brit crawled around behind me and whined. Eventually Albert fell over the edge and Angus went over on top of him. Bob began to cry. Albert came back in with a bloody nose and Angus went off to the side of the lean-to and threw up. Dan came back and Bob started telling him his life story, how his family hated him and he'd never done anything right in his whole life. "All I'll ever be is a drunk," he said after about every third sentence. And he was sobbing the whole time too.

"I'm sorry I invited you to this." Hugh said. "We're stuck here with these guys and I'm not sure I dare fall asleep. I'm afraid one of them might decide to throw up on me or something."

"I guess we can't leave them here without a way back," I said, "But why can't we go off someplace else to sleep?"

Without a word Hugh grabbed up his packbasket and headed for his boat. Brit and I followed. The others didn't even notice. We rowed to a sandy beach not far away and slept under our overturned boats.

CHAPTER TWENTY

Hugh and I tried hard to get the guys moving the next morning but we didn't get everyone home until noon. I had planned on a trip to Blue to talk to Jenny, but my time was too short. It was Sunday, so I stayed on at Hugh's the rest of the day and that night.

At night when we were in bed I said, "Hugh, where does Bob get his liquor. He's never had any money."

"Tom buys it for him."

"What about when Tom's gone?"

"You know Moose's?"

"Sure."

"Well, I think Tom has an account there and Bob can just get what he wants. Tom pays for it when he comes back."

"I have an idea Hugh."

"Hm." I could tell he wanted to go to sleep, but I had to talk this out with him.

"I'm thinking I could hire Bob to work for me this winter. He would do the easy stuff for me, so I could make more boats. He'd have a place to sleep and food and I'd pay him. It wouldn't be much but it would be more than he gets from his father."

Hugh rolled over onto his back. "That would probably be the best deal Bob has ever had."

"And maybe I could teach him how to make boats. Anyway, he'd be away from Tom and his father both. Maybe he'd have a chance to find out he can do something."

"Sounds like a great idea for Bob; I think he'd do it in a minute," Hugh said. "But is it a good idea for you?"

"What do you mean? I'd be able to make more boats."

"Maybe. But you're used to being by yourself and doing pretty much what you want. It'll be a lot different if you've got someone living with you."

I laughed at him. "Oh that's not a problem. I always wish I had more company in the wintertime."

"Okay," he said and rolled back over on his side. "I hope you remember I warned you."

I was very excited about my idea for Bob, but I didn't have a chance to do anything about it for weeks. I had clients and work to do at home, garden work mostly. And I had to get in wood. That would be another thing Bob could help me with.

The one thing that was worrying me was telling my father. I didn't know if he would appreciate having someone move in. I had to ask him first. When I finally talked to him about it he surprised me with his answer.

"Go ahead," he said. "It probably would be good for Bob to get away from his father. Just don't be too disappointed."

"What do you mean?"

"Bob's an alcoholic. It's pretty hard to reform an alcoholic, downright impossible if he doesn't want to change. You may keep him away from his home without any problem, but if you try to keep him from his liquor, watch out. You may find he won't be a friend for long."

I was a little surprised by that. I hadn't thought of Bob as an alcoholic. He was only sixteen. But I thought of the party we had at Long Lake and the way he had watched the bottles. I thought he was trying to side with Hugh and me on the drinking issue but just couldn't stand seeing those bottles pass by him. I guessed maybe my father was right.

I wondered about my father. Was he an alcoholic? Would he turn on someone who tried to reform him? I wondered if Elizabeth had tried.

But I had his approval. The next thing I had to do was talk to Bob about it.

It was into September when I finally went up to Long Lake to look for him. I figured it must be getting pretty cold in that barn at night. I wandered by his house first, trying to spot his father. He was behind the barn working on something. He wouldn't see me if I went to the door. I wasn't so worried about the brothers, but I did hope Bob's mother was the only one there.

She was, and she looked at me nervously like she was expecting bad news.

"I just stopped by to see if Bob's around," I said.

"He ain't here." She was trying to shut the door, but I was standing against it.

"Do you know where I can find him?"

"Try Moose's."

I thanked her and let her shut the door.

Moose's was a bit of a walk from Bob's. It was well after noon when I got there. Moose was at the bar and two men were sitting at one of the tables playing checkers. I didn't see Bob.

"What can I serve you," Moose asked.

"Nothing. I'm looking for Bob Parsons. Any idea where he might be?"

"Check the annex. It's over there but you have to go around outside to get in."

I went outside and around the building in the direction he'd pointed. There was a lean-to like addition with a door just an inch or two higher than my head. I knocked. There was a sound from the inside, not a come in, more like a grunt. I walked in.

Bob was lying on a very narrow bed. There was just room for the door to open and for me to walk between the bed and the wall. I had to bend over as the wall on that side was only four feet high. The room smelled of urine.

"Will!" Bob sat up on the bed and swung his legs over. "What are you doing here? Sit down, sit down." He was smiling, so I guessed he was sober.

"Your mother said I might find you here. What are you doing in this place?"

"It's all I've got. The old man kicked me out and

Tom Jackson said he'd pay my rent here until I found a job. I know you don't like Tom much Will but he's been a real friend to me. I don't know what I'd do without him."

There were a lot of things I would have liked to say about Tom and his good heart, but Bob was always so pitifully optimistic that I hated to knock him down.

"Have you found a job?" I asked.

"No, it's the wrong time of year. You know that, Will. Everybody's closing up, the sportsmen are going home. I've been thinking I should try to get a job with one of the lumbermen. They're the only one's working in the wintertime. I ain't got no traps."

"I work in the winter. I've got orders for as many boats as I can make. I thought if I had a helper to chop wood, pound tacks, do some sanding, I could get more work done. I couldn't pay you a lot but you'd get room and board free. If you want I can teach you how to make boats."

"Will Chadwick, are you offering me a job?"

"That's right."

"You sure? I ain't never done that kind of work before."

"You can split wood can't you, and keep a fire going?"

"Of course."

"We'll start there. When can you come?"

"Right now."

He put on his boots, grabbed his coat and an empty pack basket, and that was all he had. I wondered what it would be like to not even have a book of your own. I felt so poor much of the time, worrying how I was going to pay for medical school, but I'd never been like Bob. I wondered what he would do with his money when he finally had some of his own.

By the time we reached the boat it was pretty late. I knew we wouldn't be home before dark. If I worked hard I could get through the first carry about sunset. I didn't want to sleep out. The nights were getting cold, and I only had one blanket.

As I rowed I told him a little about Elizabeth and Clarissa and how we would be kind of stuck there for a while when the ice was freezing and during spring break up. Bob had always lived near town on the road. I didn't know how he'd take to being isolated. The news didn't seem to daunt him; he was so thankful to have a place to live.

We got back late as I'd expected. The lamps were out in my father's house. I made a fire in the stove and fried up some venison from the deer we had hanging in my father's shed. That was all we ate, but we were both happy to get it.

In the morning I fixed pancakes and bacon. When we'd eaten I hauled some lumber out of my loft and gave Bob the job of making himself a bed.

I might just as well have made it myself for he had no idea what to do, and I had to be running back and forth from what I was doing outside to the bed he was making inside. Finally I gave up and went inside to work on the boat I had going. That way I was right there where I could watch him and answer his questions.

I soon realized that nobody had taught Bob to wash before eating or even to wash at all. He seemed a little embarrassed when I told him he needed to bathe at least once a week and wash his clothes as well. I gave him some clothes I'd grown out of, so he would have something to wear when his own were being washed. They fit him better and were warmer than his own.

When Bob's bed was done it was a foot lower than mine because he had to keep sawing the legs off to get them even. I had to remember what I was like before I apprenticed to Mitchell so I wouldn't lose patience with him. Just because we were the same age didn't mean we had to know the same things.

We had two extra mattresses up in my father's loft. I took one down for Bob's bed. We were a little short on blankets, so I pulled out an old bear skin someone had given to my father and Elizabeth when they got married. It was supposed to be used for a rug but Elizabeth never liked it and was glad to give it up. Bob was really pleased with it for some reason and fussed over it like we'd given him the best thing we had.

My bedroom was plenty big enough for two beds. I had shelves up on all of the walls and the one wall without a window was nearly all shelves. I had books on most of them, but I cleared one off for Bob. He had nothing to put on it, but I figured it was only fair he have some space.

I was finishing up a boat right then but stopped to cut out the ribs for the next one and put him to work sanding them. He worked at it hard enough but he seemed nervous and unable to concentrate on one thing at a time. Even his conversation was choppy and didn't always make sense. He got up often to get water or go to the privy. His friendly optimism seemed strained.

Finally I asked him if something was wrong, if he didn't like the work or I wasn't feeding him enough.

"Oh, no, Will, you're being good to me, real good to me. I'm grateful, really I am."

"All right, I know you're grateful, but why do you act like you're about to explode?"

He sighed heavily and began to pace again. He seemed just about to say something for at least half an hour. Finally he said, "You won't understand, Will. You're a strong person, educated. You've got your own business. You're just a completely different kind of person from me."

I laughed. "What do you mean educated? You are the one who's been going to school all this time. I haven't been since I was nine. And you got good grades, too."

"That ain't the point, Will, and you know it. It's like you're from another class of people, like you're royalty, and I'm a peasant."

I tried to keep my face from showing anything, but the truth was, that's pretty much the way I'd always felt about Bob. He just wasn't in the same class. I said, "It's my British accent that makes you feel that way. This is America, we don't talk about class here. My father makes a living trapping and guiding, your father farms. I don't see the big difference."

"Come on, Will, your father's a doctor and everybody knows it."

"Maybe so, but don't be talking about it around him. For some reason he doesn't like it to be mentioned. Anyway, what does all this have to do with you pacing all day? You're wearing out the floor."

He looked down with a frown like he really expected to see worn spots in the boards. "It's the drink, Will. Since I started I ain't gone more than a day without it. I can't think of nothin' else. I just can't explain to you what it's like. I thought this would be a good way to stop, get away where I can't get it. But I can't do it, Will, I just got to have some."

"You can't work if you're drunk."

"I don't need to be drunk. I just need one or two drinks."

I remembered what my father had said about trying to reform an alcoholic. "Al right," I said. "how about if I go across to Kenwell's and buy a bottle from him. One or two drinks should give you about a week on one bottle. I'll deduct the cost from your pay."

"Will you do that? I don't have no money. I'm at your mercy, Will. I can't even get back to Moose's unless you take me."

"Yes, I'll do it. But you have to try to keep it to no more than two drinks a day. I can't afford much more than that."

"I will, I promise. But would you go now, Will, please."

I went, and Ike Kenwell gave me a worried look.

"Since when have you taken to drinking, Will," he said.

I suspected he may have heard about my trip to Inlet with Tom. I laughed. "Don't worry about me, Ike. I don't plan on taking another drink for the rest of my life. I hate the stuff." I told him about Bob.

He shook his head. "You've taken on a job for yourself. Good luck."

I bought two bottles, thinking that would keep Bob longer and I wouldn't have to buy any for maybe two weeks. When I rowed in Bob met me. He was going to drink some right there but I protested.

"If you drink from the bottle you won't have a measure of how much you drank. When I said one or two drinks I didn't mean half of the bottle. Tom Jackson may have an unlimited amount of money but I don't. This stuff is expensive."

"Sorry, Will. I'm gonna try, really I am. I don't want to be just the town drunk all my life."

We went up to the house and made an agreement on what size his drinks would be. He could have two a day but he was supposed to try to get by with just one. Then later on he would cut down to maybe one every other day. He took his drink and I set the two bottles on his shelf.

The rest of the day went well enough. Bob kept the fire going and I cooked. He made reasonable progress with his sanding.

I usually worked until the light wasn't good for it anymore then I fixed supper. Later, by the light of an oil lamp, I read. I was studying chemistry because it was my weak point.

Bob didn't have anything to do. He lay on his bed for awhile then got up and poked at the fire. He paced around a bit then lay back down. I tried to get him to read one of my books, but he wasn't interested.

When I finished my studying Bob was under his blanket and bear skin with his back to me. I assumed he was asleep, so I put out the light without saying anything to him.

The next morning when I awoke Bob was still asleep and there was a faint smell of whiskey in the room. I didn't think much about it but went about my morning business. When I had breakfast cooking I went in to wake him up.

The light was coming fully into the room and shone onto the two bottles on Bob's shelf. One of them was empty. Well, nearly empty. He had left maybe one or two mouthfuls in the bottom.

I ate my breakfast and let him sleep it off. When he got up he apologized for sleeping so late.

"Is there anything left to eat? I don't know why I slept so long, I really don't. You should have woke me up, Will."

"Bob, you drank a whole bottle of booze. Why did you drink the whole bottle?"

"I didn't drink it all, I left some."

"Some! If you keep drinking like this you'll use up the whole winter's wages in less than a month. Not only that, you'll have to spend so much time sleeping it off that you won't even be earning any wages. Then where will you be when the winter is over, and I go back to guiding. You'll be right where you were before, no money and no place to go and nothing to do."

He hung his head. "I don't see no other way, Will."

"What do you mean. You could save your money and buy traps or I could teach you how to build boats, and if you worked here for a couple of years you'd have enough money to build yourself a shop."

He looked up at me and that optimistic look came back to his face. "You're right, Will, you're right. I just have to try harder. I'll go two days without a drink to make up for the bottle. Then after that I'll just drink a little each day. Maybe I can drink a little less each day till I'm off it. I'm really gonna try, Will."

After he ate I sent him off to look for dead logs to use for firewood. "Go up Sucker Brook and if you find any float them on down to the mouth. We can go later and drag them back to the house."

He took the axe and left. I thought maybe if I kept him outside and busy he wouldn't have a chance for a drink. And maybe he wouldn't think about it as much either. When he was gone I hid the full bottle in the loft. I felt bad that I didn't trust him with either the bottle or my boat.

That night I heard him looking through things after I had gone to bed. The noise above me woke me up. He didn't find it though. I could tell because he woke early and was nervous. I sent him off into the woods again. I changed the hiding place just in case he'd remember all the places he looked and dig a little deeper.

CHAPTER TWENTY ONE

Ned came over that day and sat and watched. While I worked. I told him about Bob.

"I was hoping you'd do the same for me, Will," he said.

That surprised me. "Well, I would do the same for you if you needed it. But you aren't broke, you don't need a place to live and you aren't an alcoholic. I can't think of anyone who needs help less than you do."

"I mean, I was hoping you'd teach me how to build boats. I'll have a little free time on my hands this winter. I wanted to come over and watch, maybe give you a hand."

"What do you need to learn how to build boats for?"

"Don't need to, I just want to. It bothers me that there's something to do with wood and I don't know how."

I laughed at him. "You just don't like it that I know how and you don't. You always thought I was a dummy when it came to anything practical."

"That's not true. I just thought all this stuff about being a doctor was silly. I didn't know then that your father was a doctor. It would have made more sense to me if I'd known that."

"Ned, if you want to you can come over any time. I don't think Bob will be around much. I may have to have him run a trap line for me just to keep him in the woods and away from the liquor. Anyway, even if he is here, you're welcome."

"Okay," he said. "Thanks." Then he sat for a while watching me work. finally he said, "I really came over to tell you something."

"Well, tell me then." I was a little worried about what he was going to say. He made it sound so important.

"I'm getting married."

"What! You're only seventeen."

"My parents want me to wait until I'm eighteen so we're getting married in the summer after fly season."

"I can't believe it. And I don't even have a girl-friend. There was a girl I wanted to see last summer, but I kept getting hung up on one thing and another and I never did get to talk to her."

"It's better anyway for you not to have a girl if you're still planning to go to school. Do you still want to be a doctor?"

"Oh yes. Guiding is getting to be an annoying job.

"Really? I thought you liked it."

"I do sometimes, if I get the right kind of people. But with the steamboats making it easier for people and the new hotels like the Prospect...I don't know how to explain it. The people are more society folk who like to look down their noses at us as rustics. We're servants, lower class. Sometimes I'd like to just leave them on an island. I hate being talked down to like I'm stupid. Nobody's going to do that if I'm a doctor.

"Oh don't pay any attention to them. They're just stupid city people. They don't know anything anyway."

I had to envy Ned sometimes. It was easy for him to feel confident in what he was and dismiss the rest as "stupid city people." He'd never been a city person. I had. I knew they weren't all stupid.

I dropped the subject, and Ned spent the rest of the time telling me about his Louisa and their plans. He stayed until Bob got back. I hoped he would come often winter. I wasn't finding Bob to be very satisfactory company. He was too much of a worry.

Bob spent two full days collecting firewood at the mouth of Sucker Brook. He came home just before dark, ate and went to bed. He didn't seem to be upset with me and I was sure he hadn't had a drink. The next day we went out together in the boat with some rope to bring home what he'd found. I rowed and he kept the logs from bumping the boat. The smaller stuff we put in the boat. We made two trips. On the way back with the second load he said, "We've got enough now to keep us for the winter don't you think, Will?"

"Looks like it to me," I said.

"Then can I have a drink when we get back."

"How much do you want one?"

"I want one bad, Will."

"I didn't mean that. I mean, do you want one more every day or do you maybe want one a little less than you did two days ago."

He thought about that for awhile. "I think it's about the same."

"But you didn't get up last night to look for the bottles like you did before. Don't you think maybe it's getting a little better."

He turned red. "Well, maybe. I was real tired last night though."

"See, maybe that's what you have to do for awhile, just work really hard and get yourself so tired you don't care. Then, after awhile the craving will wear off."

"I don't know, Will, I want a drink real bad."

"Why don't you just try it another day."

I had the bottles and the boat and the money. There wasn't a whole lot Bob could say about it. I kept putting him off day by day and he seemed to be doing fine. He did plenty of work for me and did it well. I was ahead on my boat building. It looked like maybe my plan was going to work out after all. I was also beginning to really enjoy his company. Brit even took to following Bob around. He was outside and about more than I and made better company for a dog.

The first week in November I decided to take a trip to Long Lake for some supplies. I was out of cornmeal and low on bacon and flour and had a list of things Elizabeth wanted also. I'd planned to leave Bob at home, but he said he really wanted to see his friends. He'd been away from home only a little more than a month, longer than ever before. He was a little homesick. So I took him. It would make things easier, I reasoned. He'd be able to help me on the carries.

I expected to stay over somewhere, probably Hugh's, so we didn't get an early start. Recently, with more people coming through, certain men had started manning the longer carries with their wagons. I guess they made a pretty good living when the lakes were open, hauling the sportsmen and all their gear from lake to lake. I usually carried my own, but this time I told old Joe, the wagon man, to keep an eye open for us the next day as we'd be coming through with a good load.

We beached in town early in the afternoon. I went in to give my order to Cyrus Kellogg so he'd have it ready for me by noon the next day. Bob said he'd meet me later; he was going to see if he could visit with his mother. He took off on foot with his empty pack basket.

I stopped in at Mitchell's first. I had to ask him for some advice on a bit of a design change I was thinking about. After about an hour there I went to Hugh's. They fed me and put me up for the night.

Hugh and I sort of expected Bob to show up there because we had no idea what kind of reception he'd get at home. He never came.

I stayed at Hugh's until about 11:00 the next morning. Bob never came so I went to Kellogg's to pick up my order. I paid for it and took it all down to the beach then I sat inside with my book and waited.

It was three o'clock when Bob came up the road, bent almost double and staggering from the weight of whatever was in his pack basket. I figured it was booze. He'd been gone too long to be just visiting his mother. Where else did he have to go but Moose's.

I met him outside and helped him off with his pack basket. Sure enough, there was nothing in there but bottles. Must have been at least sixty pounds of it. Bob was sober, but I could tell he'd been drinking hard the night before. His face was red, especially around the eyes and he acted dead tired. Of course he had come several miles with quite a load.

"How did you afford all that stuff?" I asked. I'd been hoping he would stay off the liquor if I didn't give him any money until spring.

"Tom Jackson set up an account at Moose's. I can get anything I want there. Tom's so rich he don't even notice."

I'd nearly forgotten about Tom. I wondered what it was he wanted out of Bob anyway. Why would he even care about him except maybe for the enjoyment of having so much control over someone.

"I thought if I got something to drink for myself you wouldn't have to worry about the expense of it," Bob said. "I know you just want the best for me Will, but you don't know what it's like to crave something so bad. I've got to have my own liquor."

I was so frustrated I nearly told him he had to leave it behind, but I was afraid he'd stay with it so I didn't. I had barrels of flour and cornmeal, two bushels of apples, bacon, lard, butter and salt, plus a few other small things. Add to that Bob's load and we'd be riding pretty low in the water. I hoped we wouldn't hit rough water in the north part of Raquette. If we did we'd have to camp and wait it out.

Joe was waiting for us at the carry with his wagon. I was glad to see him.

"I'd about give up on you boys," he said. "Another half hour and I'd have gone home for my supper."

We loaded our supplies on, then the boat, and Bob, Brit and I sat on the end of the wagon as Joe's horse pulled us to Forked Lake. We would still have to haul everything over the carry from Forked Lake to Raquette. We rested while we could.

By the time we got all our supplies to Raquette it was past dark. But the lake was calm. I was mightily relieved about that. I didn't look forward to a night of keeping the varmints from my food.

I was really annoyed with Bob. He'd made us late then brought along that extra, worthless load for us to carry. Everything turned out all right though. When we got home my father was still awake and he helped us unload and carry everything up. But I was still really put out. What if things hadn't gone smoothly? What if old Joe had gone home early? What if the lake had been rough? I wished I could go home to my own house and have the place to myself. Hugh had been right; I wished I'd listened to him.

Bob went inside to start a fire in the stove. I followed my father to his house and told him the whole story.

"I don't know what you're complaining about," he said. "Everything turned out all right."

"But Bob took off and got drunk when he said he was going to visit his mother."

"What did you expect?"

"Well, he hadn't had a drink in about a month. He could have been cured. If he'd gone a whole month he could have kept on without any alcohol."

"He went a month without because he didn't have a choice. It was what you wanted him to do. You can't trick someone into giving up an addiction. Sounds to me like you're just mad because your plans for Bob didn't work out. He hasn't done anything to you."

I muttered that I wished I could have my life to myself again and left. I should have known better than to complain to my father. After all, he was an alcoholic, too, even though he didn't admit it. Of course he would take Bob's side.

When I went inside Bob was frying up some venison and he had that talkative optimism that I realized had been missing for awhile.

"I know you're mad at me, Will, but I'll do my work, you'll see. I had to have my drinks. I just go crazy inside without them."

After we ate he took a candle into the bedroom and arranged all of his bottles on his shelf and counted them. "Twenty bottles," he said. "That should see me until freeze up. Then I can walk home three or four times a month. That way you won't have to buy none for me, Will."

He made it sound like he was doing me a big favor.

I couldn't stay mad at Bob long. He was good with Clarissa and Brit loved him. He did his work well enough. I didn't teach him much about boat building. I didn't trust him with a lot of the finer work, and he didn't seem interested anyway. He liked trapping and helped my father out when he got the chance and when I needed him to do it.

It was Tom I hated. Bob could never afford to drink if it weren't for Tom and I was sure he'd been the one to get Bob started on it. For all his meanness, Bob's father was not a drinker, nor were his brothers. Tom, the rich boy, had nothing better to do than take pleasure in buying people's lives or working hard at making other people look like fools.

CHAPTER TWENTY TWO

That winter, besides dealing with Bob and making boats, I was studying hard. I wanted to be ready to take the entrance exam as soon as possible. I was not sure I had enough money for school though. Elizabeth had mentioned to me several times that I shouldn't worry about it. I tried to pin her down about why. But she would never tell me anything more. I assumed she thought that the Graysons were planning on helping me. But no one had come out and offered me help so I didn't dare expect any.

In late April, after the ice went out, I took Bob back to Long Lake and paid him. I worried about him because he still had no place to live. But he couldn't stay on with me. I would be guiding again soon and he had no boat. I wasn't sure what the summer would bring, but if I could manage it I hoped to be in school next winter.

Ned got married late in June. He moved into a house he and his father built on the north side of Constable Point.

He wasn't the only one who got married that summer. Mr. William West Durant married Janet Stott. Everyone was in quite a tizzy about the whole thing. They were by far the richest people on the lake and that made it an interesting story. They took off on some long, exotic honeymoon.

I wished I had a girlfriend, but I was glad I wasn't getting married.

The summer did not start out well for me. The first party I guided knew nothing about living out of doors or being on water.They called me "boy" and questioned everything I said. It was a real struggle to be nice to them and even more of a struggle to keep them from hurting themselves and my boat. I wanted very badly to say, "If you gentlemen know so much about it you don't need me," and leave them. But they would have been stranded.

There was a steamboat on Raquette Lake now. It was becoming far too easy for these society people to get to the lakes and there was enough luxury and company of their kind to keep them there.

I was mightily grateful to leave my two clients at the steamboat landing on Utowana Lake.

Two days later I rowed into Long Lake and began asking around about Bob. He'd been seen around looking like he'd been drinking heavily. Nobody was sure where he was staying. So I went to Moose's.

Bob was there all right and so was Tom. They were sitting at the bar. I couldn't see Tom's face when I went in but Bob was staring at him with that optimistic look on his face. He looked small, like a little kid almost. There were things I wanted to ask him, but none of them did I want to talk about with Tom listening. I was considering slipping out again when Tom turned and saw me.

"Well, hello there. Here comes the little white hunter. What brings you into the man's domain?" He was being very loud as usual, trying to get the attention of the several other men who were there.

"I came to visit Bob," I said. My voice had a peevish sound and I wished I could be more casual and under control in these situations.

"Oh yes," Tom said, "I heard you tried to make an honest working man out of Bob. Aren't you even smart enough to know you're wasting your time?"

"What are you talking about," I said. "He did a good lot of work for me this winter."

"That may be true, but he'll always come back to me because I have what he needs. I've got lots of money, and I give him all the booze he wants.He needs to drink and I'm the only one who's going to give it to him. He'll do anything I tell him."

"I don't need to buy my friends."

If he noticed the insult he never showed it.

"That may be true. But you've got no control over them. I have complete control over Bob." He slapped him on the shoulder.

When I looked at Bob he had such a look of helpless humiliation that I couldn't bear to stay. I turned around and walked out.

"Better luck next time boy." Tom was laughing, but no one else was.

I felt so bad I couldn't even talk to Hugh about it. I couldn't help but feel there must have been something else I could have done for Bob to keep him from having to hear that. I wished mightily I had never gone to see him.

For the next few weeks I was consumed with an absolute hatred of Tom. If I had seen him again and had my gun with me I believe I could have shot him.

I told my father about the conversation and what he said surprised me.

"You know, Will, if you become a doctor you'll have to care for people like Tom. And you are going to have to be as concerned for their health as you would be for Bob or Hugh or Ned."

"I wouldn't save that man's life. He's evil."

"That's not for you to decide."

"Do you treat everyone who asks you?"

"Of course. Have you ever seen me refuse to take care of anyone?"

"No."

"Of course not, and I'm not even a practicing doctor. But if someone is sick or hurt and they haven't got anyone better to take care of them I'm under obligation, because of my knowledge, to help them."

"Why aren't you a practicing doctor? Wouldn't it be a better way to make a living than guiding?" I'd wanted to ask him that for years. And now that I had I was not sure I wanted to hear the answer. I was sure it had something to do with my mother.

"I'm not dependable enough. If someone puts their life in your hands you have to be there for them. You have to follow through."

"Why can't you?" I was still angry about Tom and it was carrying over to my father. What reason could he give me that I had to be the son of a trapper instead of the son of a doctor? What reason that I had to live a life of humiliation?

"I'm an alcoholic, Will. Surely you know that. I may not drink all the time but, just like Bob, I always want it. I wasn't there when your mother needed me. Sooner or later it would happen again. That's why I don't like people to know."

I'd suspected it for years, but I never expected him to come out and say it. I hadn't suspected that he always craved a drink. Was he really like Bob?

Hearing him say that made me feel alone and scared. What was it that could have that kind of control over my father. Bob was small and weak, but not my father. I wanted to cry. I just nodded to him and left his porch where we'd been sitting.

I went into my own bedroom and lay down. Bob's short and slightly crooked bed was still there on the other side of the room. I wondered if I'd done everything I could have done for him.

I wondered if I really wanted to be a doctor. All my life the world had seemed big and full and bright. Now it felt small and tight. If nothing could be done to help my father or Bob, what good was medicine. I remembered how my father had told me doctors couldn't do much. Now I understood.

I slept and in the morning I was still confused. After so many years it was hard for me to give up a dream all at once. I was prepared and quite sure I could get into a medical school. But now I wasn't sure I wanted to. Although I had two professions, it made me feel lost to think of being only a boat builder and a guide the rest of my life. I wanted to go to school. I wanted to make money and I wanted to be respected. But I also liked the idea of being able to heal people. Was there really enough of that in the business to make it worthwhile?

I ate my breakfast and set out in the boat to cut a spruce knee I'd marked three weeks before.

When I came back I noticed my father was still home. I wrestled the wood out of my boat then pulled the boat up and went to talk to him. He was working in the garden. I got a spade and started working on the potato patch. He had the seed potatoes cut in pieces and lined up on the grass.

"I've been thinking maybe I shouldn't become a doctor after all," I said.

"Why not? You'd be good at it. If there is one thing you aren't it's undependable."

I was surprised. I didn't expect him to bring up yesterday's conversation, and I'd always thought he didn't want me to be a doctor.

"You used to say a doctor couldn't really do much. I'm beginning to think you're right. Besides, I don't have the money. I still want to go to school, but I don't know what I want to do."

He stood up and leaned on his spade. "Son, I think this would be a good time to tell you that you don't have to worry about the money. We've got the money."

"Are the Graysons going to pay for it?"

"No, Will. You know your grandparents were very wealthy. When they died their money was split between your Uncle John and myself." He went on digging.

I was stunned. "You mean we've been rich all this time--since I was ten?"

"Yup."

I was too shocked to be excited. "All this time?"

He just nodded.

"Why didn't you tell me?" I was beginning to be angry.

"Why did you need to know? A young boy doesn't need money."

"Everything would have been different. I wouldn't have had to do all this stuff."

"What stuff?"

"You know, guiding and making boats."

"I didn't know you didn't like doing those things."

I was feeling a little confused. I tried to think of not being able to make boats. "It's just that I wouldn't have had to put up with all these society snobs looking down their noses at me."

"I think, more often than not, people look up to you because of what you know and what you can do."

"Maybe. But if I'd known I had money I wouldn't have had to do anything."

"Oh, you would have liked to be like Tom Jackson? I didn't know you admired him that much."

That made me mad. I grabbed my spade and stalked off. My father never had understood the import-ance of money. Yesterday I'd felt so bad for him because he was trapped by his alcoholism. Today I was angry. How could a man who was so educated fail to under-stand the importance of having people look up to you.

I went into my house and looked around. All my boat making tools were put away because it was summer and I was guiding. What if I had known I was rich? Would I have learned how to make boats? I thought about the knee I'd brought home earlier. I needed to get it out of the weather where it could season. I went out my front door and saw the tent lying there. I needed to sweep it out and get it ready. Tomorrow I had patrons to pick up at Blue, and I had to take the tent. I went down for the wood and hauled the heavy thing up into my loft. Then I cleaned up the tent and folded it.

This was ridiculous. I was rich and I had all this work to do and obligations right through the summer. And for the past seven years my father had trapped and guided and planted and made syrup and hauled in firewood when he didn't have to.

I filled my pack basket with the things I needed for the guiding I'd be doing all week. Brit watched and wagged his tail. He loved going out on the job. When I finished all my preparations I grabbed the spade and went back to the garden where my father was still planting potatoes.

"Why do you do all this hard work when you don't have to?" I asked. "Why do you sleep out in the rain and cold and bugs and put up with people calling you things like their "mighty servant" when you don't have to? Why do you trap?"

He didn't answer for a bit. He placed a row of seed potatoes in their holes and began hilling up around them. "Oh, for you I guess. And your sister. It just doesn't seem like a man can be a good example to his children without some kind of work to do." He stood up, stretched his back and grinned. "Now that you mention it though, I think it may be time to retire from the trapping. That cussed cabin up there gets colder every year. Maybe I'll have to take up painting or writing or maybe whittling."

"What about Elizabeth? Don't you think she'd like to live in a little bit more luxury. She's use to it."

"That's just it, Will; she had plenty of luxury in her life, for that matter so did I. Look at your Grandfather Grayson. He can have anything he wants and when he gets free time what does he do? He comes up here and fishes and cooks for himself and helps me chop wood, anything he can do for himself he'll do. Not everyone thinks the best way to live is to sit around and pay other people to do things for you. What good is life if you don't have anything to do and don't know how to do anything?"

I was still a little angry, but I thought about my boats and the pleasure I got from seeing someone row by in one of them.

I had plenty to think about on my slow, quiet trip up Marion River. My frustration with alcoholism had been overwhelmed by the sheer presence of money. But I still had to struggle with the question of whether I would become a doctor. I didn't need to.It was purely a matter of whether I wanted to.

I didn't think much about Bob or Tom that summer until I crossed Tom's path at Long Lake. He was pulling his boat up on the sand near Kellogg's. It was not the one I'd made. It was a newer one and looked like one of Mitchell's, but it had some deep gashes in the ribs and a scratch in the paint on the siding.

"You know that boat you made for me Chadwick," he said.

I didn't answer. I hadn't made any boat for him.

"It just didn't hold up. I think you've got a serious problem in your construction technique. Had to get a new one."

It occurred to me that Tom wouldn't even use a boat if his parent's house wasn't across the lake from town.

"Say Chadwick, while we're on the subject of failed careers, whatever happened to that idea you had that you were going to become a doctor. I haven't heard much about that lately." He was sneering at me, waiting for an answer.

"What about your career?" I said. "Shouldn't you be pretty close to being a lawyer by now?"

He laughed. "Oh, that's just a diversion Chadwick. I don't have to work. I have money. I'd rather leave the work for people like you."

Not long ago I'd have yearned to be able to answer him back with fantastic tales of how rich I was. Now, for some reason I could not understand, I didn't want Tom to know I had money.

"That's fine," I said. "I like work."

I pushed my boat out and headed for home. I'd just finished a job and had three weeks with no work to do. By the time I reached the first carry I knew what I was going to do. Elizabeth and Clarissa and I would go spend some time with the Graysons. I could visit the medical school there and see what I had to do to get in.

I thought about Bob and wondered if he was staying in that room off Moose's. I wished I could do something for him, but after I'd seen him humiliated so much I wasn't sure I ever wanted to see him again. It might be too embarrassing for both of us.

I was at the end of the carry and I lifted my boat above my head to set it in the water. Off to one side was a battered looking boat that I recognized as mine, the one Tom had misused so badly. It had a large tin patch on the starboard bow just under the water line. One of the ribs had been patched together with a metal brace. I was inspecting the patch when Bob stepped out of the woods.

"Is this yours?" I asked.

He was smiling, but it was a different sort of look than he used to have. He looked less optimistic and more realistic. That's the best I can explain it.

"It's mine. Tom left it off at Mitchell's when he picked up his new one. It was a sorry mess, but Mitchell patched it up. Harry told him I was looking for a boat, so he gave it to me for a dollar."

I was surprised. Not that he had the boat but that he had a dollar to pay for it.

"Why didn't Tom just give it to you."

He looked pleased that I had asked. "Oh, you haven't heard?" he said.

"Haven't heard what?

"That day in Moose's last spring, you know; the day

Tom made that speech about owning me. Well, I guess there ain't anybody so low that they can't be pushed too far. That was too much for me. I ain't had a drink since. I ain't seen Tom since neither. I've had to work real hard to avoid him but I've done it."

"That's the best news I've had in a long time," I said. But how are you living?"

"Living in lean-tos mostly. It's been better since I got the boat. When you paid me I gave all the money to Cyrus Kellogg and told him I'd come get supplies when I needed them. I got me this old gun use." The gun lay in the bottom of the boat wrapped in burlap. "I've still got credit, and I plan to get some traps. I'm out here now trying to find me a good trap line."

"Where will you live?"

"I thought I could get a small log shelter thrown up before winter."

It made me cold just to think of it. "Maybe you could talk to my father. He told me he might not trap this year. If you ran his line you could live up at Shallow Lake. That cabin wouldn't be bad if it had a stove in it."

"That's an idea," he said. "I'll poke around Forked Lake and see what I find then maybe I'll go down and talk with him."

"You should do that," I said. "Good luck. And congratulations."

I went on home and found my father working on the chicken house. I told him about Bob. "Dad," I said, "Do you think I should be a doctor?"

"I think you'd be a good one. You have staying power, a sense of responsibility and you're good with your hands. What do you think?"

"Well, I guess just because a cure for something hasn't been found yet, it doesn't mean we should give up trying. I sure will miss making boats though."

"But you won't miss trapping."

"I pledge to never walk a trap line again."

Made in the USA
Charleston, SC
29 June 2014